PICTURES

LOIS SIMMIE

Fifth House

SASKATOON, SASKATCHEWAN

1984

Copyright © 1984 Lois Simmie

Reprinted 1989

Canadian Cataloguing in Publication Data

Simmie, Lois, 1932 -
Pictures

ISBN 0-920079-08-3 (bound)
    0-920079-06-7 (pbk.)

I. Title.
PS8587.I43P5   1984   C813'.54   C84-091120-3
PR9199.3.S54P5   1984

ACKNOWLEDGEMENTS

Some of these stories have appeared in the following publications or been aired as indicated:
Romantic Fever, GRAIN, *Best of GRAIN*, CBC Anthology; Red Shoes, *Saskatchewan Gold*; Pictures, GRAIN, CBC Anthology; Emily, *Sundogs, Canadian Short Fiction Anthology Vol. II*; The Long Way Home, CBC Ambience, CBC Anthology; Mick & I & Hong Kong Heaven, NeWest Review.

This book has been published with the assistance of the Saskatchewan Arts Board and The Canada Council.

Printed by
Hignell Printing
Winnipeg, Manitoba

Cover: "Hound Among the Poppies"
by Marie Elyse St. George
from the collection of Saskatchewan Telecommunications

Fifth House Publishers
20 – 36th St. E.
Saskatoon, SK
S7K 5S8

CONTENTS

*To my sister, Betty. And to all the friends of Bill W.,
for their experience, strength and hope.*

ROMANTIC FEVER

For a long time Amy thinks she is sick because she
fell off the dray. Sometimes it's mixed up with the nickel
she didn't put on the collection plate, she bought a bag
of candy with it after church and Reverend Black told
them sinners were always punished. She didn't always
hear what Reverend Black said because he looked so
much like a tall grey rabbit, even his eyes were pink,
from crying over sinners, Amy's father said.

She remembers coming home that night after she fell
off the dray, the bad pain in her knee spreading to her
ankle, her other knee, her wrists. Monica walks with her,
talking and talking. Amy wants Monica to stop talking,
she wants to lie down in the snow.

"Were you riding on that dray again?" Her mother

1

pulls off her snow-crusted ski pants and jacket in the back porch. Amy is nearly ten, and her mother has not undressed her for a long time. She keeps wanting to lean against the cold wood wall. Her little brother Billy appears in the kitchen doorway in his pyjamas, lifting first one foot and then the other away from the cold floor, his round brown eyes staring. Mackenzie, their cat, named after Mackenzie King, rubs around his feet.

"Were you on the dray?" her mother asks again.

"Yes." It hurts everywhere her mother touches her, everywhere the clothes touch her.

"Wait until I see Alfie Sears. He should know better than to let you kids ride that dray, he's no better than a kid himself." She jerks at the jacket sleeve and a pain shoots through Amy's shoulder. She can't stand up any longer; she slides to the floor, puts her hot cheek against a rough, cool two-by-four. She feels her mother's strong hand on her forehead. It feels so good, so cool, she wants to fall into it, lie down in it, be wrapped up in it, but she is growing very large and the hand is getting smaller, a tiny, hand-shaped dot on her huge forehead.

She is in bed, the covers cold and heavy, hurting her skin, and she shakes until she goes rigid, hands, feet, eyes clenched, there is not one place that doesn't hurt. A big man in a curly fur coat and hat stoops under the sloped ceiling, the doctor, doctor, doctor, her mother is saying, came on the jigger, her mother is wearing lipstick, where is she going? They squeak down the stairs, going on the jigger to get Amy's father who ran away away away, her mother and the doctor will chase him on the jigger, chase him down the track, he's running between the rails, his plaid jacket billowing behind him like a sail, his red hair gleaming in the moonlight; his hair, the rails, her mother's lipstick, all gleaming in the moonlight.

The doctor is back, pushing a thermometer between her teeth, pressing something cold and hard on her chest. He doesn't see her father and the lady with the black hair and the glittering earrings, her father is wearing a fur hat and coat and they are dancing around the foot of her bed and up the sloping walls, she is wearing a fur hat and coat and they are dancing around the foot of her bed and up the sloping walls, she is wearing a red dress, laughing and dancing as light as dandelion seed. Amy is so glad he is there she doesn't even care about the lady, doesn't care that watching them dance hurts her eyes.

She wakes up in her parents' room at the front of the house. A strange woman in a yellowed white dress is sitting in the wicker chair by the window reading a Bible. She turns and looks at Amy with mean little eyes. "Praise the Lord," she says.

The room is very crowded with Amy's white iron bed against the wall about two feet away from her parents' big bed, the dark dresser with the round mirror against the wall by the windows, the tall matching chest against the other wall. A foot or so above Amy's bed the wall angles up, covered with large pink cabbage roses. Her parents' wedding picture hangs by the window, and on the other side there is a picture of a curly-haired, rosy-cheeked girl sitting under a tree with a basketful of rabbits. One of the baby rabbits is nestled on her blue skirt which is spread out on the grass. Amy doesn't remember them moving her bed in here, but she likes this room, larger and sunnier than her own, where her mother sleeps now.

Miss Bolt, the nurse, sleeps in the big bed. Every day she rubs Amy's arms and legs with peppermint-smelling liniment and wraps them in scratchy red flannel. Her hands are hard and rough. Every night she twists her mousy hair in strips of paper, turns out the light and stands looking out the window at the church across the street, her knobby head and white nightgown outlined by the streetlight outside the window. She kneels between the two beds and says her prayers out loud; she always prays for Amy, prays she won't die in the night, then she climbs into bed and starts to snore. Amy hates her.

Her father is in the room, kneeling by her bed, sobbing. He smells of other places. He puts his head down on the bed and his springy red hair tickles Amy's arm.

"My baby, my poor, poor baby," he sobs. Amy feels as if she is at a picture show. Miss Bolt's pale lips are tight. "You will upset her. Her heart," she says.

He straightens up and strokes Amy's hair, but her hair is in fuzzy, tight braids, so that is not as nice as it could be. She wants to hug him but feels shy with Miss Bolt watching.

"But whoa now!" he says, wiping his eyes and smiling, "I brought you something." He is wearing his good brown suit with the vest and looks very tall and handsome as he stands up. He goes out and comes back with a celluloid doll on a stick. The doll has blonde wavy hair, round blue eyes, and is naked except for a lot of fuzzy pink feathers, a string of pearls, and a gold cardboard top hat. In one dimpled hand she carries a shiny black cane, and in her ears are tiny pearl earrings. It is the most beautiful thing Amy has ever seen.

"It's a kewpie doll," he says, handing it to her. She touches the downy feathers, softer than anything she has ever felt, except maybe the lighter grey fur behind Mackenzie's ears.

"You buy them at carnivals," he tells her, kneeling beside the bed. She has heard of carnivals. Something like a fair. They went to the Battleford Fair once and she got sick on the merry-go-round, throwing up on the man who lifted her off the wooden horse at the end of the ride. She wants to ask her father where he has been to a carnival but she can not. She also cannot ask him if he is home to stay.

Miss Bolt attaches the doll to the side of the big mirror because she thinks it is bad for Amy to do anything; she must lie as still as possible. Miss Bolt once had a patient, a man, with rheumatic fever who ruined his heart forever because he sat up in bed one day and yelled at her. Miss Bolt always looks happy when she tells this story. It's all right about the doll because now she can see it from the front and the back. When Amy gets better she will build a stage for the kewpie doll and put on shows; she will make curtains for the stage out of some red velvet pieces her mother keeps in a trunk. She spends a lot of time thinking about how she will do it.

Monica comes, bringing her a bottle of Evening in Paris cologne and a Crispy Crunch chocolate bar.

"Phew!" Monica says, wrinkling her nose. "You smell funny."

"It's wintergreen liniment."

"You look funny, too, wrapped up in those red rags." Amy has forgotten about them. She has spent all her life wrapped in red flannel. She thinks she would feel strange without it.

They share the chocolate bar, licking their fingers and picking up the crumbs from the wrapper. Monica looks different, her dark hair has been cut in bangs. She has a new cat called Snoopy, she wishes Amy could see it. She got ninety-six on a spelling test. Clarence Saunders stole Joyce Thibault's pen and the teacher made him give it back in front of the whole class. Reverend Black says all the kids who have perfect attendance at Sunday School will get to go to church camp at the lake next summer. Monica has perfect attendance.

"You sure look different. White and skinny," Monica says. Amy is surprised, no one else has told her this. After Monica goes, she turns her face to the wall and cries a little. She feels white and skinny; even her tears feel puny.

Amy wakes up from a nap. Reverend Black is sitting in the wicker chair by the window, his rabbity profile turned towards her, looking out the window at the church as if he is afraid something might go wrong while he is not there.

"Hello, dear child," he says, when he hears that she is awake. "And how is our patient today?"

She is tired of people asking that, she is the same as she is every other day.

"I hate being in bed," she says.

"Tsch, tsch," his sad pink eyes regard her. "We mustn't hate God's will." He says it like God swill.

"I can't help it," she says.

"Ah, not a very patient patient." He smiles, showing his pale yellow teeth. She hears her mother banging pots in the kitchen. The radio in the front room downstairs is playing "Praise the Lord and Pass the Ammunition." He reads from the floppy black Bible on his lap: "I said, I will take heed to my ways that I sin not with my tongue; I will keep my mouth with a bridle, while the wicked is before me . . ."

Amy stops listening. She remembers her father saying, "How can you take someone seriously who looks like a bloody rabbit?" Amy's father went to church at Christmas and Easter. "I kept expecting him to hop over and start nibbling the Easter lilies," he said once. Amy smiles, remembering. She thinks about the bag of candy she bought with her collection money and decides she will do it again the first chance she gets. So now she has another sin to think about; she hates God swill. She doesn't care, she just wants him to go and leave her alone.

He finishes reading and goes, leaving behind a faintly musty smell, like the church.

"Bloody rabbit," Amy says. "Bloody damn rabbit."

"Billy, stop that! You're getting on my nerves." Her mother's impatient voice reaches up the stairs.

Poor Billy, he is lonesome. He has no idea what to do with his time now that he doesn't have Amy to tell him. When they played war, Billy was the Jap who got shot down in flames. When they played house, he was the baby, always put to bed in the wagon and covered up to his nose — even on hot days he never complained. And when they had a funeral, Billy was the corpse. Sometimes Amy or Monica would be the dead person; Amy thought she was much the best at it, folding her hands on her chest and jutting her nose in the air (the way her grandmother had looked in her coffin), but sometimes it was so sad she shed a few tears and Monica said it looked stupid for the corpse to cry. Billy was a pallbearer or a mourner then, and he was quite good at it, wiping his nose and eyes with one of their father's handkerchiefs and sniffing a bit. Almost every day now, Amy hears her mother yelling at him to for heaven's sake go out and play. Miss Bolt doesn't like him coming into her room, but he sometimes sneaks in when she is downstairs.

One afternoon, Billy comes in while Miss Bolt is having coffee.

"Let's play Japs, Amy," he says. She nods with her eye on the door while he climbs onto the big bed and happily revs up the motor of his Jap fighter plane. He whooshes and swoops all over the bed, arms stretched out to the side, while she shoots at him. "Ackackackack-ackack" she says, he loves that, but under her breath so Miss Bolt won't hear. When she hears her coming, she whispers fiercely, "kerPOW! Direct hit!" and he falls face down on the bed and stays there all afternoon.

Eventually he falls asleep, looking happy, his eyelashes very dark on his red cheeks. Looking at him reminds her of the song she hears so often on the radio about the white cliffs of Dover, ". . . and Jimmy will go to sleep, in his own little room again." Amy feels sad every time she hears the song though she doesn't know why.

She worries about the war crossing the ocean while she is sick in bed, worries that her father will not be home to carry her away somewhere, somewhere where the bombs aren't falling. Worries that her mother might be visiting and not get back in time. Maybe Alfie could take them on the dray, galloping through the night, runners gliding quietly on the snow, softly calling to Jess and Babe, "giddee up, giddee up", softly so the Germans and Japs couldn't hear. She would feel safe with Alfie. She wonders if they would have to take Miss Bolt.

The second time Monica comes, a long time after the first, she brings a purple and pink plant. It is a coleus, she tells Amy. Her mother sent it.

She talks about Janice, Janice's new doll, Janice's new blue dress with three frills on the skirt, Janice's baby sister. There are long silences.

Some time later, Amy hears Monica and Janice playing on the street in front of the house, their voices sharp and piercing in the spring air. They are playing a game Amy made up. "Who goes there?" shrieks Janice, "Friend or enemy?" She is supposed to say friend or foe.

Miss Bolt has started going home two days a week to cook for her old father and wash his clothes. One night late when Miss Bolt is not there, Amy wakes up to a faint tinkling sound, like windchimes; clothes hangers, bumping together. In the dim light from the streetlight, her father is stooping beside the low, open closet, carefully pulling things out and putting them in a paper shopping bag. He is wearing his good brown suit. He lights a match and in the shadow from the flame he looks deformed, even his face looks different. He says "shit!" when the match burns his fingers. He tiptoes to the dresser and pulls open a drawer very carefully, stuffs socks, underwear and handkerchiefs in the bag. Amy thinks of Santa Claus. The kewpie doll on the mirror smiles down at him.

A little later the front door closes softly and the car starts with a loud, coughing noise and sputters away down the street. It speeds up when it turns onto the highway and the sound gradually fades away. It is very quiet. The front door bangs open, there is a rush of feet on the wooden walk, "Good riddance!" her mother screams into the silence. Later her mother comes quietly into the room and takes the wedding picture down from the wall. Amy hears the sound of breaking glass from her mother's bedroom. She thinks about Billy. She will ask him to come in and play tomorrow.

She gets a valentine from Monica and one from Alfie Sears. Alfie's card says: Roses are red,
Violets are blue,
You better get better
Cause I miss you!!!
It is signed, "your friend, Alfie Sears. p.s. I have roman-

tic fever, too. haha.'' Her mother reads it. She shakes
her head and smiles. "Ronald Coleman," she says. Amy
remembers her mother's friend saying Alfie wore a moustache and let his sideburns grow long because he thought
he looked like Ronald Coleman. Her mother tucks the
valentine in the mirror frame opposite the kewpie doll.

Mackenzie is wrapped around Amy's neck, purring.
Her mother lets him on the bed on the days when Miss
Bolt is home with her father. Miss Bolt will not even allow
him on the bed. She doesn't like cats, which doesn't surprise Amy. He is lovely and soft and warm, and his purring is so loud it feels as if it is coming from her own
throat.

She knows it is officially spring the day the dray
lumbers past the house, on wheels, banging and vibrating
like thunder over the holes in the road. She pictures him
there, legs spraddled and rooted to the dray as if they
are growing out of the smooth wood. He holds the reins
loosely in his big hands except when he slaps them on
the horses' round rumps. Miss Bolt is looking down out
the window and she shakes her head and clicks her
tongue.

"That man has no sense of responsibility," she mut-
ters; even her pale nose looks disapproving. Amy decides
to grow up with no sense of responsibility.

"Amy! Amy!" Billy's hoarse whisper from the door.
He is standing there with Mackenzie draped over his
arm, and Miss Bolt is somewhere in the house. His eyes
and cheeks are bright with the excitement of the daring
thing he is doing.

11

"Bring him here," Amy says. She, too, is becoming more daring. Mackenzie pats her nose, tugs on her braid, while Billy sits on the other bed, looking pleased with himself.

"When is she going home?" he asks.

"Pretty soon," says Amy, who doesn't really know, has been afraid to ask, afraid she may never go. "Pretty soon," she says again.

"Daddy called her Lightning Bolt," he says. Amy laughs but her throat feels thick.

Billy lies down on Miss Bolt's bed and tucks his hands under his head, elbows jutting out like angel wings. He crosses his legs and his boots leave black smudges on the white chenille bedspread. Mackenzie is restless and wanders down to the foot of Amy's bed.

"What means orders, Amy?" Billy asks.

"Telling somebody what to do. Why?"

"Miss Bolt takes orders from the doctor, she said."

"Uh huh."

Mackenzie lifts his tail toward Amy and meows loudly.

"I'm going to be a doctor when I grow up," Billy says.

A great wriggling tangled mass of worms erupts from under Mackenzie's tail, falls to the bed, still writhing. Amy screams and claws her way onto the other bed, scrambles over Billy who bawls "Ow, Ow, Amy!" Then she is past him and he sees the worms, more are coming, they keep coming and coming. Billy shrieks, a high, piercing shriek. Thundering steps on the stairs, Miss Bolt in the room, sharp eyes taking it in, Mackenzie is jerked up by the neck in one hand, the cover stripped off in the other and she's gone down the stairs and out the back

12

door, Billy still shrieks, hanging onto Amy's neck, nearly choking her, his hot tears spurting onto the front of her flannelette nightgown.

"Be quiet, Billy!" She is trying to hear what is happening. She is shaking all over and her heart flops around in her chest like a frog in a jar.

Her mother heard the commotion from next door and runs into the room, sweeping them both into her lap. She hugs them to her as if she needs their comfort, their protection, as Miss Bolt puts things to rights, fury in the quick beating of her rubber soles on the floor, the snap of clean sheets on the other bed. Amy doesn't look, doesn't have to, she feels Miss Bolt's mean eyes on the back of her neck.

After supper, her mother comes and kneels by Amy's bed. Her eyes are red and puffy. Miss Bolt says they must get rid of Mackenzie, he is bad for Amy. She will not change her mind, will leave if they don't, and the doctor says she must stay a while longer. She holds Amy for a long time and then gives her a backrub and tucks her in. When she has gone, Amy turns to the wall and cries. She cries as she has never cried for her father, or her grandmother when she died, as she has never cried for anything, ever before.

The day Miss Bolt leaves for good they have a party. Amy's mother makes a chocolate cake with thick chocolate icing and brings a plateful upstairs. They sit cross-legged on the big bed; Amy in her plaid housecoat, her mother in an old housedress with bare legs and feet, Billy in dirty overalls and his mother doesn't even make him

take his boots off. They laugh a lot and their mother reads
"The Shooting of Dan McGrew," with lots of feeling.
When she reads the part about the miner sitting down
to play the piano "with scarcely the strength of a louse,"
she gives a very good imitation of a weak louse, rolling
her eyes and going limp all over, and Amy and Billy
roll on the bed and laugh till their stomachs hurt. A piece
of chocolate cake gets mashed under Billy.

When she gets to the end — "but the lady who kissed him and pinched his poke, was the lady that's known
as Lou" — Billy says, "What's his poke?" and their
mother laughs until she flops back on the pillows and
says she cannot, simply *can not* get up.

She sleeps in the big bed with Billy that night, holding
Amy's hand across the space between the two beds until
they fall asleep. Just before Amy goes to sleep, she hears
her mother whisper to the room, to no one in particular,
except maybe Miss Bolt: "And we're getting another
cat. So there."

Her mother helps her up every day and lets her sit
by the window and read. She watches the kids playing
and sometimes talks to them through the screen. "When
are you coming out?" they ask, squinting up at her, and
she tells them she will be out soon. "Gee," they say
respectfully, "my mother (or dad, or teacher) says you
were really sick." And she starts to feel just a tiny bit
important. Monica stops to talk, brings her new doll
under the window so Amy can see, tells her to watch
for her in the Germany Surrender Parade.

"I'll be glad when you can come out and play," she
says.

"Want to come up and play with my kewpie doll?"
Amy asks.

And then one day she is ready to walk again. To try
to walk. She can't believe how weak her legs are — like
trying to walk on strings of cooked spaghetti. Her mother
holds her on one side, and Alfie Sears supports her on
the other side, with a solid arm around her back. He
is very tanned already and his white teeth look even
whiter when he smiles. He is warm and strong and Amy
leans into him.

"I'm going to carry you downstairs for supper," he
tells her. He has been coming to visit her, and always
stays and has coffee with her mother, staying for supper
sometimes. She hears them laughing in the kitchen. He
brought her a ginger kitten two days after Miss Bolt left.

They relax their grip and she takes a couple of shaky
steps by herself, then Alfie holds her again. Billy jumps
up and down on the bed: "Ay-mee's walk-ing! Ay-mee's
walk-ing!" he chants in time with his jumps. He is
holding the ginger kitten under its front legs and it
squirms down and skitters away, back hunched, and falls
off the bed. They laugh.

Amy looks at her mother, seeing how thin she is but
still pretty when she is smiling, as she is now, her brown
eyes very large and shiny. She puts her arms around her
mother's neck and hugs her; she would hug the whole
world if she could. She feels the warm spring sun on her
face, and the floor is warm under Amy's bare feet.

RED SHOES

"I'll get Lazybones out of bed while you finish that up."

Through the screen door, Meg saw her father coming up the path, his walk jaunty, his long arms swinging. He was wearing a light blue shirt and tan pants she hadn't seen before.

"I'm up," she said, moving closer to the door.

Now she could see her mother, bending over in the garden, Carson standing beside her with one long skinny leg tucked up like a stork or flamingo. Mom was dressed up, too. They must be going soon.

"I'm not in bed," she said, feeling guilty. She shouldn't have slept in this morning. They shouldn't have let her.

He was in the kitchen now, smiling at her. She'd be happy, too, if she was going to Kentucky instead of to the farm where there was nobody to play with but Carson, not even any animals except chickens and they were no good for anything.

"We'll only be gone three weeks," he said, as if he'd read her mind. Three weeks.

He dipped some water from the pail on the cupboard and drank thirstily, spilling a little on his new shirt front. She could smell the newness.

"It's going to be a hot day," he said, putting the dipper back on its nail. "Cheer up."

He tweaked one of her braids. He smelled of soap and clean morning air and she wanted him to smell of engine grease and grain dust, because then he wouldn't be going anywhere. She gave him a little hug to show him she loved him even if she was mad at them for going without her. He felt the same even if he smelled all wrong.

Then her mother was in the kitchen, holding the dishpan full of vegetables away from her so she wouldn't dirty her white polka-dotted dress. She was flushed and smiling, she looked happy, and that was so unusual that Meg let go of her father to stare at her mother. Carson was peering through the screen, still standing on one leg, her brown bangs hanging in her eyes. Her mother washed her hands in the basin, drying them briskly on the towel that hung over the pump handle like a flag at half mast.

"There," she said. "There was no use leaving these in the garden to rot. Carson, run them over to Mrs. Hartley's now, but don't dawdle. We'll be leaving soon."

Carson opened the screen and hopped over to the cupboard. She picked up the pan, executed an awkward turn, and hopped back out the door and down the steps. Her mother laughed.

"I wonder how long she's going to keep that up."

Meg felt a stab of jealousy. When she had tried to do everything with one hand after being at Aunt Laura's, her mother had said it made her feel like screaming. Aunt Laura had lost an arm while she was still a baby in Kentucky. And when Meg cut herself trying to peel a potato with one hand, her mother *had* screamed at her. But because it was Carson it was all right. Or maybe it was because she was getting along better with Dad, it was awhile since Meg had heard them fighting in the night.

"How soon will you be ready?" Dad asked. He was leaning against the cupboard with his arms crossed.

"Oh . . . fifteen minutes." There was a lilt in her voice.

"Good. I'll finish packing the car."

The screen door whapped shut behind him.

"Meg, I've laid out the clothes I want you to wear to Grandma and Grandpa's. And please don't argue, everything else is packed." She hurried out of the kitchen, the white dress swishing around her bare legs, then her quick, light footsteps pattered on the stairs.

Through the screen Meg could see her father, out by the car. He was standing back from the trunk as if he expected something to jump out at him. *The sun shines bright on my old Kentucky home*, he whistled, as he rearranged something in the trunk, *tis summer, the darkies*

19

are gay. And suddenly, in his new clothes, he was someone other than her father, someone who knew about gay darkies and blue grass and hard times a knockin' at the door. Blue grass. He swore it was, and he didn't lie, but still she could hardly believe it. *WeeEEP no more MY laDEE,* he whistled, slamming the trunk shut.

Carson hopped around the corner of the house, her face all screwed up with concentration and just the tip of her tongue sticking out. You could tell she was getting tired but she wouldn't stop. Carson was stupid. Meg turned away from the screen, not wanting to see how she made out hopping up the steps. ''Stupid,'' she said under her breath as she ran for the stairs.

In the car on the way to the farm, their mother was laughing a lot, turning often to look at her and Carson. Somehow it reminded Meg of the time they'd gone to Biggar to see the king and queen, except that then Meg was excited, too. She hadn't even minded being squished in the back seat with the Wylies; she'd just sat there imagining the trailing robes trimmed with spotted fur, and the jewelled crowns they'd be wearing, like in the picture over the board at school. And the six white horses that would pull the carriage through town.

It was awful, though. They were just standing there on a kind of iron porch at the back of a train and they looked like ordinary people, the queen was even wearing a blue hat like her mother's. The king wore a dark suit and looked like he had a headache. Dad said the king looked like that because the war was coming. Meg wondered why they just didn't stay home then, and get ready, instead of riding around on a train looking gloomy, with everybody waving flags at them, trying to cheer them up. On the way home in the car, Jackie Wylie threw up on her.

Old Tom, their grey cat, dozed nervously on the seat between her and Carson. She hoped he wouldn't run away at the farm like he had one time, and she couldn't stop touching him, though Carson kept saying not to, to let him sleep. Meg couldn't remember a time when they hadn't had Old Tom.

Her mother was talking a lot to her father now, more than she had for ages, asking questions about Kentucky and all his relations there. She kept putting her hand on his shoulder or the back of his neck, and Meg could tell the way he kept turning and smiling at her that he liked it. Carson nudged her and they grinned at each other. Their mother was acting the way Joyce Hartley acted when that homely Harry Wilkins sat with her on the Hartley's front porch. It was almost worth missing them for three weeks to have things the way they used to be.

She twisted in the seat and smiled back at them. There were little sparks of red in her brown hair. "What would you like us to bring you?" she asked.

"A new dress," Carson said promptly, adding, "if that doesn't cost too much." Errh, that Carson, always saying things like that to show people how grown up and good she was.

"And how about you, Meg?"

"Some blue grass," she said, and then because that sounded silly, even sillier than Carson, she said, "Red shoes." Jean Wylie had some red sandals her aunts had brought her from the States. "Red *sandals*," Meg added,

21

feeling proud of being so precise, and suddenly knowing that's what she wanted more than anything. Mom smiled and said she'd see.

Meg felt excited for a few miles, looking at her old scuffed brown oxfords, mentally replacing them with shiny red sandals. Carson was crazy, you could get a blue dress anywhere, Grandma could even make you one, and would if you only asked, but you couldn't even get red shoes in Eaton's catalogue.

"These crops are looking darned good. That wheat should go forty bushels at least, if there's no hail," her father said. He knew about these things because of running the elevator. Meg loved the dim, raftered elevator, airy and loud with birds. She liked the feel of gritty grain on the wood floors, golden wheat spilling from trucks, the chug chug chug of the engine, like an immense heartbeat in the middle of town. She liked the sound of men's voices shouting over the noise of the engine, their dusty, sunburned smiles, the creaking lift that could carry you up to the top of the elevator, the top of the world.

"Maybe we can make some wheat gum at Grandpa's" she said, and Dad said yes, the wheat should be just about right for gum.

"But don't chew up all of Grandpa's crop," he said, winking at her in the rearview mirror.

Meg laughed and then she suddenly wanted to cry. She had to stare hard out the window at the blurry fields and trees, until the ache in her throat went away. She mustn't cry when they left, Carson had told her and told her.

And she didn't cry when they left, watching from the

upstairs balcony as Dad waved frantically out the window, like someone in trouble, until the car was out of sight. Then Grandma called them to crank the handle on the ice cream freezer. Making ice cream was something she did only on really special occasions.

When the ice cream was done, Meg and Carson took a pile of National Geographic magazines up onto the balcony, and in the ivy-shaded corner by the chimney, they looked for pictures of Kentucky, but there weren't any. They had to sneak the magazines up there because Grandpa didn't want them looking at pictures of head-hunters' wives with long narrow busts hanging free in the sun.

The weather was suffocating, heat pressing down from a clear blue sky day after day until the monotony blurred the days together the way a heat mirage shimmered road and sky into one on the horizon. Walks to town a quarter of a mile away for Grandpa's plug of Club; the hot, velvety dust of the road burning the soles of her feet and puffing up between her toes, no sound but the wind sighing the crops, a meadowlark's call, and the humming of the telephone wires looping along beside the road. Meg imagined her grandmother and Mrs. Findlay talking, their voices thin strings of sound in the hot blue afternoon.

It was good to see people in a particular place when you thought about them, that's why it was so hard with them in Kentucky, she'd only seen pictures of big-toothed aunts and uncles standing in front of some extravagant tree that went up and up right out of the picture, trailing strings of lacy leaves to the ground. She looked at the dusty wolf willow bushes beside the road and tried to imagine a tree like that, but it was almost as hard as seeing blue grass.

She had no trouble seeing the shoes they were probably buying right that minute — the gleaming red leather and shiny buckles, the new red smell of them. She thought of them whenever she thought of Mom and Dad.

Most of all, whenever she was alone, she liked thinking about how happy they were when they left, so now she didn't have to worry that Mom might leave and take Carson, like she'd heard her say once when they were fighting in the night. She'd been afraid to leave the house for days, terrified of stepping on a crack or doing something else that would make it happen. Step on a crack, your mother won't be back.

Carson nearly drove Grandma crazy with worry, hopping all the time.

The first time they helped her weed the garden it was so hot she made them wear hats and long sleeves, and it was horrid work, the dry dirt packed tight around the roots, hanging on for dear life. Carson was hopping between the rows, sometimes losing her balance and stepping on the radishes or carrots. Grandma straightened up, tucking a strand of grey hair back into its bun with a grimy, green-stained hand.

"Carson, please don't do that, you'll injure yourself." She was frowning as if she were trying to understand why Carson was doing it. "I'm afraid you'll put your hip out of place."

Carson just pressed her lips together and changed to the other foot.

"Won't you please stop? For me?"

Carson shook her head and her eyes filled up with tears.

"Please?"

"I can't," was all that Carson would say.

Grandma went into the house and then Grandpa was coming out past the lilac hedge, storming down between the rows, his old purple and grey checked sweater flapping around his hips. He wore it even on the hottest days. He'd just woke up and he looked mad.

"Stop that!" he roared, though Carson was just standing there staring. "By the Lord Harry, if the Lord had meant ya to hop, he'd have only give you one leg!"

Carson was so scared that she hopped over the beets. Meg knew she didn't mean to that time.

"What the Sam Hill do ya think ya are?" Grandpa yelled. "A kangaroo? Eh? Even a kangaroo knows enough to hop on two legs." He squirted an amber jet of tobacco juice into the corn and glared at Carson. "You'll stop that confounded hopping or I'll take the razor strap to ya and then you'll dang well hop!"

Grandma had come out and was standing a little way behind him, looking sorry that she'd told him. Grandpa turned on her.

"Why the Sam Hill didn't they take these kids with them?"

"Now Paw," Grandma said.

"Well? Why didn't they?" He looked mad at her, too.

"They just wanted to get away by themselves, I guess. I can understand that." Grandma was crumpling up her apron, smudging it with dirt.

"Ya think I can't?" he said, as if he hadn't asked the question. He scowled at them. Meg was standing behind Carson, trying not to be noticed. Then she bent down to pull out a weed and pulled out a beet by mistake.

"Look at that!" he hollered. "Useless little tits, can't tell beets from weeds." His face was red and his moustache quivered and he looked like he wanted to hit something. He kicked at a cornstalk and broke it off.

"See?" he yelled at Grandma. "See what they made me do? I've a good notion to take the razor strap to both of them. Town kids!" he said. "They're no danged good for anything."

"Don't say that, Paw," Grandma said. She looked ready to cry.

"Don't tell me what to say." He gave her a long look and then he turned around and started back toward the house. At the lilac hedge he stopped and looked back to where they were all standing as if they were rooted in the garden like the cornstalks. "And I seen ya looking at them dirty pictures. Little preeverts." He disappeared behind the hedge.

"What's a preevert?" Meg asked, and Grandma started to laugh, the same kind of laughing Meg had done in the car when she really wanted to cry. She looked like Mom when she laughed like that, with her head tipped away back and her eyes squeezed almost shut.

Carson stopped hopping so much after that. The hard black razor strap hung on a nail by the kitchen washstand and they had slapped themselves on the hands and bare legs to see what it felt like. Just a little smack hurt like everything. Besides, when Grandpa wasn't sleeping you never knew where he was, peeking out the tool shop window, or hiding around the corner of the house, trying to catch her at it. "Stop that!" he would roar suddenly from some unexpected place, and Carson would nearly fall over from fright.

Grandpa mostly slept away the hot afternoons on the old horsehair couch in the dining room, his hands folded on his chest and a large, bony hump in his nose that Meg never noticed any other time. He complained of chest pains, and swallowed turpentine from a bottle in the kitchen cupboard for toothache. Grandpa's chest pains mostly came on him when there were weeds to pull or water to haul from the well. Meg and Carson took turns with the water, carrying two pails half full suspended from the wooden yoke that was carved to fit your shoulders. Grandma said they'd go to the lake when Grandpa felt better but he never did. He said jumping around in that cold water just gave people the rheumatism, anyway.

Old Tom disappeared and she and Carson became inseparable then, calling and calling him, looking everywhere he might have got shut in — in the cool, sawdusty ice house, the milk house with its faintly sour smell though there hadn't been cows for a long time, the empty barn, and the shop where Grandpa spent most of his time amid the tangle of tools and wire and things that needed fixing.

"Here kittykittykitty," they called, till it seemed to echo back from the empty sun-baked buildings, the dusty trees. "HERE kittykittykittykitty," until it echoed inside their heads. They even opened the cover on the well, holding their breath as they leaned over and peered down and down to where the dark water gleamed, a hollow, damp "kittykittykitty" rebounding in their ears. Meg dropped Grandpa's flashlight in and it hit the water with a low, echoing splash, the light spiralling lazily down under the water until it disappeared.

They were so afraid of what Grandpa would do that they rolled on the ground and laughed until they cried.

"By the Lord Harry I'll take the razor strap to ya!" Carson shrieked, falling over in the long grass and pounding her fists on the ground.

"What the Sam Hill do ya think you're doing?" Meg shouted, kicking her legs at the sky, "you'll give my flashlight the rheumatism!"

He never looked for the flashlight, though, because it stayed light so late.

Late one night she heard Old Tom yowling under her window. Carson heard him, too, and they collided on the landing in a tangle of arms and legs and the smell of sleep. There was a jagged tear in one of his short ears and a deep scratch, already beginning to heal, on his soft, grey nose. His purring filled the kitchen.

Carson lit the coal oil lamp, they were beyond caring about Grandpa and the razor strap, and they fed him, sitting on the floor on either side of him, marvelling at his wounds, his beauty, his *thereness*. Loving him. Loving each other.

There was only one postcard from Mom and Dad, and Meg worried as she lay in bed at night with the moths bumping the screen and the Findlay's dog barking in the distance. Kentucky was a place where terrible, exotic things happened to people.

28

There was Aunt Laura losing her arm, (they always said it that way, "Laura lost her arm," as if she had just misplaced it somewhere); there were poisonous spiders, and Dad's baby brother who burned to death when his nightgown caught fire in the upstairs fireplace. The part of this story that fascinated her even more than the baby burning up was the idea of having a fireplace in the bedroom. Maybe they were there right now, looking at the fire. Or walking arm in arm on that blue, blue grass. She always went to sleep thinking about the red shoes, how she'd walk down the street in them and everyone would know they came all the way from Kentucky.

And then, late one night, she woke up to the sound of her father's voice downstairs. She listened, straining her ears, until she heard her mother laugh. Carson's running footsteps passed her door and pattered down the stairs. She wanted to go, too, but a strange shyness prevented her. Finally she crept out of bed and down a few steps to the landing where she could crouch down and see into the sitting room.

Carson was standing close to Mom's chair, Mom's arm around her. In the soft light from the Aladdin's lamp Dad's face was tired, and the sadness was back, even when he smiled at Carson. It was there, too, in the droop of his thin shoulders under his old tan shirt. Meg held onto the staircase, peering between the rails, wanting to be down there but unable to move. She could hear Grandpa snoring in his room at the head of the stairs.

Mom was telling Grandma about the heat in Kentucky and the scorpion she'd found hanging on the bedsprings and how Aunt Kit had killed a black widow spider in the car right over Mom's head. It had a red hourglass on its belly.

"Did you bring the dress?" Carson asked.

Mom smiled. "Yes, we brought your dress."

"Did you get Meg's shoes?"

"You bet we did," Dad said, trying to sound jolly. "We went all the way to Bowling Green to get those shoes."

Carson was jumping up and down. "Can I wake Meg?"

"Well, you won't be able to sleep without seeing that dress, will you?" Dad said, but Carson was already running for the stairs. Meg made it up the stairs and into bed before Carson jumped on her.

"Meg! Meg, wake up, they're home. Mom and Dad are home."

"Mmmmmm?" She tried to look convincingly sleepy.

"Get up, get up. They've got our presents."

Then they were coming up the stairs, lamplight spilling ahead of them, were in the room, bending over her bed, smiling and talking in low voices so as not to wake Grandpa. They looked different, somehow, not as she had imagined them all this time, her father thinner, with white strands in his sideburns she had never noticed before, her mother's hair cut short and she was wearing new red slacks and red earrings. She looked like somebody in a Good Housekeeping magazine, somebody who might be in a story there, sitting on a train with a soldier, or smiling and holding a refrigerator door open in a bright, modern kitchen. It was hard to look at her.

Dad went out to the car for the presents and Grandma

sat on the foot of the bed, patting Meg's suddenly cold feet, squeezing them in her soft, warm hands. Her long grey hair hung away down the back of her old blue robe. Dad came back with the parcels. Carson's dress was in an exotic blue bag with PENNY'S on the side. Carson spread it out on the bed. It was as blue as a bluebird's wing, with an enormous full frill and a long sash that tied behind. There were pink and green flowers embroidered on the chest.

Carson ran into the closet, leaving the door ajar, and came out in the dress. Oh. Oh. Not even in Eaton's catalogue had there ever been anything like this dress. Meg's hand was stayed inside the shoebox on her lap as she stared. Carson twirled around and the skirt flew out, filling the room like a royal blue tent. The puffy sleeves had pink flowers embroidered on the cuffs. It was a good thing Carson slept with her pants on under her pyjamas because the dress lifted straight out from the waist, but even her baggy pink pants with the hole in the bum couldn't spoil the dress.

"Open your shoes, Meg. Try them on." Carson was jumping up and down on the bed now, flickering the flame in the lamp chimney.

Meg folded the tissue paper back and lifted out one gleaming red shoe. A sandal with two straps and shiny silver buckles, little holes cut in the leather over the toes in the shape of flowers, a teardrop-shaped hole for each petal.

"Try them on, try them on." Carson, whirling the skirt over Meg's head like an immense blue parasol.

Grandma relinquished Meg's foot from her warm grip

and went to get a clean pair of white socks. The shoe
was for the left foot and slid on perfectly.

"Perfect," her mother said, doing up the buckles and
pinching the toe. "They'll last you for awhile."

Oh God, it was beautiful. It looked, felt, it even *smelled*
beautiful. Dad was smiling at her, happy for her. He
was stroking Old Tom who had appeared from somewhere, attracted by the rattle of the paper. Her mother
unfastened the buckles on the other shoe and Meg took
it, started to put it on.

No. Oh, No.

She squeezed her eyes shut. PleaseGodpleaseGod-
pleaseGodAlmightyFather Son and Holy Ghost please
make it not true. She opened her eyes and looked, but
it was true. The shoes were both for the same foot. She
threw the blanket over her head, threw herself into the
pillow, and howled.

Late the next day Meg limped barefoot toward the
barn, carrying the shovel and the shoebox. Old Tom
followed a little way behind. She had forced her feet into
the shoes and worn them all day and now there was a
great bleeding blister on her heel and more starting to
form on the toes of her right foot. Carson caught up with
her and they walked together in silence.

Behind the barn Meg dug the hole, longer and deeper
than it needed to be. Carson watched, so did Old Tom,
and Meg was glad they were there. When the hole suited
her, she set the box in it. Then she reached in her pocket
and pulled out the dry grass Dad had brought, blue grass
that wasn't even blue, just an ashy grey color, and she

opened her hand and let it drift down onto the box. Then she took the shovel and covered it up.

On the way back to the house she realized that Carson was crying.

"It's Grandpa's fault," Carson said. Tears ran down her face and dripped off the end of her chin.

"What is?"

She was still thinking of the shoes, wondering how long it would be before she would have to dig them up again, try to make them fit.

"What's Grandpa's fault?"

"He wouldn't let me hop till they got back, and this morning I heard them fighting again." She wiped her chin with the back of her grimy hand. "If he'd only let me do it till they got back, everything would have been all right."

And Meg was not surprised. Somehow she had known it all the time.

PICTURES

Sundays were all the same. The dray didn't rumble
down the street to meet the train, Rose Flodell didn't
shake her mop out the back door with her hair tied up
in one of Jake's old handkerchiefs, the hitching post in
the front of the livery stable stood empty. In the fierce
heat, the false storefronts on Main Street had a stiff, en-
during look. Sunday was worse in the summer — hot,
still, interminable.

That Sunday was like all the others. Stuffed into a
church pew between my mother and my brother, Lloyd,
I watched the dust motes swirl lazily in a shaft of sunlight,
and stared at the back of Mrs. Wilson's hat. It was made
of peacock feathers looking out in every direction, like
huge, judging eyes. God's maybe. Ellen Wilson, my best

friend, sat beside her mother, her hair so tightly french-braided that it pulled the scalp out in little white points in a couple of places. Next to Ellen was Mrs. Potter, the butcher's wife, the fine, black veil of her hat pinned securely into her brown doughnut of hair. A bug — a bedbug, I was sure — had crawled out of the ring of hair and was pushing against the veil, first here, then there, trying to get out. I squeezed my mother's leg hard, pointing urgently up at Mrs. Potter with one finger, but she took the hand by the finger and put it firmly back in my lap. Mr. Potter exuded the faint smell of fresh blood and sawdust through his heavy black suit.

During prayers, my vision was confined to my mother's flowered lap, and Billy's fat thighs, which threatened to burst their flannel skins like overstuffed sausages. My mother's church hands were, in their idleness, so unfamiliar that I would cast surreptitious glances at her face, finding it as strange and closed as the hands. I knew one Sunday we'd be caught forever in this state of suspended animation, unable, one Monday morning, to go out the door to school, to work, my mother too weak to empty the heavy pails of water into the boiler on the stove, to carry the basket of wet sheets out to the clothesline.

During those dreary services, heavy with the smell of piety, the only person who looked like her weekday self was Maryann Flodell, sitting on the floor in the aisle with her chunky legs splayed out in front of her, surrounded by wax crayons. As the rest of us obediently rose to sing ''Stand up, stand UP for Jee-zuss'' in a draggy tempo, or got prayed over till our necks ached, Maryann stayed

right where she was. She wasn't about to stand up for
Jesus or anyone else when she could sit and draw.

She dropped the pictures around her like scattered
jewels on the drab, wood floor. Incredible scenes. Yellow
skies, blue trees, red suns. Fantastic animals peering
through blue foliage and hanging from the branches:
blue-eyed, green tigers, extravagant orange lions, crimson snakes, and Beula, their pet goat. She always made
Beula white, with black horns and hoofs.

Maryann was "simple," people said, or, "the porch
light is on but nobody's home." To me, Maryann was
just Maryann, we had lived next door forever. We were
both eleven that summer, though Maryann was already
"developing," my mother said, as if she were a negative,
and I was hard and thin as a stick.

After church, Maryann skipped among the people,
her round face beaming, her little hooded eyes almost
disappearing in her bunched-up cheeks. She swung on
her mother's arm while Rose talked to my parents. In
a blue dress and red veiled hat, her black hair already
springing out of its Sunday roll, Rose was just as nice
to look at as Maryann's pictures, with the same feeling
of too much energy to be contained inside a border.
Somehow just looking at Rose always made me feel good.

Jake Flodell never came to church, he spent Sunday
morning on their rickety back steps, mournfully nursing a hangover, and grooming his pet goat. Rose said
he'd gone to church once or twice but always felt like
he was going to faint. I envied Jake this strange infirmity.

Jake worked on the CNR section gang, arriving home
most Saturday nights roary-eyed drunk. He would come

floating down the street, singing lustily, his scarecrow body moving with a kind of grace he never possessed while sober, his protruding brown eyes full of a wild, happy light. Sunday night he walked back up the street, eyes bloodshot, clothes hanging as if he'd lost ten pounds since the night before, and took the jigger out of town for another week of pounding rails or whatever it was he did out there.

He won the goat in a poker game and brought it home one Saturday night, with the idea of milking it some-day, but they never did. Rose wanted to sell it, but Jake became fond of it and wouldn't give it up. He couldn't bear to have it dehorned, so it went around butting things, knocking Jake or Maryann ass over teakettle every so often, and eating everything in sight. Mostly it spent its time sprawled on top of a shed at the back of their yard, inspecting the neighborhood and bleating nastily at my mother whenever she went outside. When she went to the toilet, Beula kept it up all the time she was inside, making her constipated.

Most everyone had dispersed from in front of the church, and Ellen had finished the handshaking ritual her parents put her through every Sunday. At least I was spared that, but Ellen didn't seem to mind people saying what a little lady she was getting to be and that sort of thing.

"What are you doing today?" she asked.

"I dunno. Nothin, I guess." It was getting unbearably hot on the sidewalk.

"Are your aunts coming?"

"Yeah. Probably." I wished they wouldn't. My father's two sisters, widowed and spinstered, came almost every Sunday. They sat primly in neat dresses and narrow shoes, talking about the weather or "Mama and Papa," my dead grandparents, in soft, hopeless voices.

"Want to go for a walk?" Ellen asked. We moved aside to let the Potters go past on the sidewalk. Mr. Potter had two fingers missing, and people always joked about who had got them in their hamburger.

"There's nowhere to walk to," I said. "And anyhow, I have to stay dressed up." Lloyd got to change into old clothes after church, while I had to stay starched and polished till after supper. My mother saw no injustice in this. "Lloyd is a boy," she would say if I complained, and believed her logic unassailable.

"We could just walk on the tracks. It's better than going home," Ellen said.

A mean-looking red ant emerged from a crack in the sidewalk and I stepped on it. "Okay," I said, feeling a little better. "There's nothing else to do."

Ellen's parents were walking off down the street, Mrs. Wilson stepping carefully, so you knew her Sunday headache had already started and she was going home to lie in the darkened bedroom with an icebag on her pale forehead. She called them her Sunday headaches, though they almost always dribbled on into Monday and Tuesday. Ellen's father held her elbow as if he were holding a fragile glass figurine.

"Yes, you two run along and enjoy yourselves," he said, when Ellen told him we were going. He smiled, showing his even, white teeth. Mr. Wilson was nice-looking. He had freckles, like Ellen, but they suited him better because his hair was red while Ellen's was no particular color.

"It's awfully hot, Jim," Mrs. Wilson said anxiously. She had very pale blue eyes that almost seemed to disappear inside her head when she had a headache.

"Then we'd better get you out of the sun, Ruby. The girls can look after themselves perfectly well." Hearing her first name could still surprise me; she was so colorless, with no flash or sparkle anywhere. And they proceeded down the street toward their Sunday afternoon, filled with icebags and pills and the fretful voice from the bedroom. Mrs. Wilson was a good woman, people said, but "sickly," and they lowered their voices respectfully in her presence, though nobody seemed to know what was the matter with her. Mr. Wilson was the druggist, and had the shiniest shoes of anybody in town.

The railroad track was no fun on Sunday. You couldn't walk the rail in slipper-soled shoes, and there was no train on Sunday, so there wasn't even the horrifying possibility of being squashed as flat as the pennies we sometimes laid on the track. Once I stayed on the rail so long when the train was coming that the brakes shrieked and the engineer leaned out the cab window, shaking his fist and swearing at me as the train thundered past, his face as red as the bandana around his neck. Sprawled in the long grass I looked up at him, and forever after thought of him as an integral part of the train — a long, motorized centaur.

We moped along the track, kicking at the ties, throwing stones at the crows on fenceposts and poplar bluffs, while the heat pushed at us from all sides. Even the crows were listless, their squawks bored, as they ignored our poorly aimed stones. Only the grasshoppers, zealously bounding over the weeds, seemed unaffected by the smothery Sunday pall.

"I'm going to pick Mother some flowers," Ellen said.

"Yeah." Ellen was always picking flowers for her mother. I used to help her, but her mother never got any better or any worse, and eventually I got bored with it. Ellen came back with her hands full of dusty fireweed and bluebells. I had picked up a stick and was smacking it on the rail with every step.

"Don't do that, it's getting on my nerves." I recognized the fretful note in her voice, hit the rail once more and then stopped.

"People go to the toilet on the train and it comes right out on the track," I said. We had had this conversation before. We'd had most of our conversations before.

"I don't believe that." Ellen was rearranging the flowers, her narrow fingers prim.

"They do, too. Lloyd saw a pile of shit right in the middle of the track." Sunday had made me reckless. "With a little square of toilet paper stuck in the middle of it."

"That's vulgar." Ellen narrowed her eyes and scrinched up her lips. "That's really vulgar." I could tell the way she liked saying it that it was going to be her favorite word for awhile.

I dragged the stick from tie to tie, trying to get some satisfying noise from it. Ellen sighed a couple of times.

Then, after awhile, she said, "You like Rose Flodell, don't you?" Her voice was too casual, and something in me stood at attention.

"Yeah. Sure, I like Rose. She's nice."

"Mother says Rose Flodell is vulgar."

"What? She is not!" I yelled, hitting the rail a whizzing crack, furious that she would use the same word for Rose and a pile of turds on the track. "Rose is nice. She's . . . *nice*!" Wanting some other word. Not knowing it. I wanted to knock the stupid bouquet out of her righteous fingers. "Don't *say* that. Rose is my friend." I wheeled around and started back, running and slipping in the smooth-soled shoes, suddenly desperate to leave the heat and Ellen's stifling persence, behind.

"Rose is bad," Ellen yelled.

I stopped and looked back at her, standing there in her neat jumper and braids and shiny shoes, holding the red and blue flowers. "It's true," she said. "Mother says Rose Flodell is immoral."

It was very quiet as I looked down the tracks at Ellen, with only the buzzing of a grasshopper and the sound of a pebble shifting by my shoe. The silence smelled of clover and some small dead thing in the weeds. I didn't know what immoral meant and I wasn't going to ask.

"At least she doesn't have bedbugs," I said finally.

"What? Who has bedbugs?" Ellen's voice squeaked up on the word bedbugs.

"You do. A bedbug crawled off Mrs. Potter in church and onto you."

Ellen threw the flowers everywhere and started tearing at her clothes. "Oh no, oh God, oh no!"

"It's in your hair," I yelled. "It crawled out of her hair onto you and up your braid. I saw it."

Ellen swatted crazily at her braids, screaming and crying and jumping all over the track.

"It crawled away up inside where it could lay eggs," I shouted. "That's what they do, you know. They've probably hatched already in the heat."

"Oh, God! Come and look!" Ellen shrieked, yanking the ribbons from her braids. "Arrrrrgh! Arrrrrrgggghh! I can't stand it!" She was running around in circles, clawing at herself. "Come and look, Jeannie! Oh, *please*, come and look!"

"I can't," I said. "Mom wouldn't want me getting bedbugs." I turned around and started home again, while Ellen screamed and bawled and carried on behind me. "Bedbugs are vulgar," I shouted over my shoulder, and was rewarded by a blood-curdling shriek. I threw the stick as far as I could and kept going.

The aunts had arrived and were fluttering vaguely around, asking my mother what they could do to help. There never was anything, but they always asked, and then went gratefully into the front room to visit with my father and wait for the savoury smell of roasting chicken. Lloyd was hunched over the kitchen table, spooning chocolate icing into his mouth, and my mother was leaning against the cupboard with a glass of water in her hand. She had the glassy-eyed look she always got when the aunts were there, and her face was flushed and shiny with perspiration. I took the pan of potato and carrot peelings from the cupboard and went out.

Jake was sitting on their back steps, his skinny legs gathered inside his arms. Beula was standing beside him, and they both turned as the screen door slapped shut behind me. Beula bleated hello. Maryann looked up from where she was sprawled in the dirt beside the steps, drawing.

"Hi Jake. Hi, Maryann." I put the pan down beside Beula and settled onto the bottom step. The brush Jake used to groom Beula lay there, full of her soft, white hair.

Jake grinned down at me. "Hi, Jeannie." He gave one of my braids a little tug. Maryann grinned up at me. She was drawing another jungly scene, a National Geographic magazine open beside her. Mr. Wilson had given her a lot of old ones, and she never got tired of looking at the pictures.

"Hot, eh?" Jake said. He dropped his cigarette end in the dirt, and reaching a long leg down beside the steps, ground it under his heel.

"Sure is hot," I said. I was glad to be there, where the shade was beginning to creep over the steps.

"Yep. Hotterna damn firecracker," Jake said, staring gloomily into the glass of cloudy liquid in his hand. Beula was peering down at me over Jake's shoulder. I never got used to her eyes, with their strange, horizontal pupils, and wondered if she saw everything sideways. I mentioned her funny pupils to Jake once, and he said they weren't any funnier than Miss Thompson's up at the school. He nearly choked to death laughing at that one.

"Want some lemonade," he asked, as if he didn't expect anybody in their right mind would, really. He lifted the glass and swallowed, his Adam's apple bobbing up and down in his stringy throat.

"Yes, please." My mother hardly ever made lemonade.

"Rose!" Jake bellowed over his shoulder.

"For goodness sake, you don't have to wake the dead." Rose's voice, and then Rose appeared at the screen door. "Hi, Jeannie." Rose always said hello in her musical voice as if she was really glad you were there. It made me feel good inside just to see her, as if I hadn't seen her for a long time. Through the screen she looked different, kind of blurred around the edges.

"Got some lemonade for our friend here?" Jake grinned up at Rose. His teeth were almost as dark as his sun-baked skin.

"I sure do. Nice and cold, too. I just got a fresh pail of water." And she disappeared into the messy kitchen. I knew it was messy because it always was, in a comfortable kind of way, with Maryann's glowing pictures pinned up everywhere. They never worried about paint the way my mother did. My mother always defended Rose's housekeeping though, saying there was nothing but clean dirt at the Flodell's. Rose had a heart of gold, she said often, and when I was younger I used to imagine it gleaming in her chest like a big, gold locket. Or those pictures of saints with little lines going out from their hearts.

"Here you are, honey." Rose came out with three glasses, handing one to me, and leaning over the steps so her breasts showed above the blue dress, she gave one to Maryann. She sat down beside me on the bottom step, stretching her bare legs out in front of her, and kicked off her shoes. They were blue and white pumps, and I

wanted a pair just like them someday. Her toenails were
polished bright red. "Holy Mother of God, it's hot,"
she said.

Beula had finished the peelings and was chewing the
ribbon on my left braid, then commenced munching on
the braid itself.

"Here! Let go! Miserable beast." Rose slapped at
Beula, who bleated pitifully. "She'd eat your head if
you'd let her." She laughed. She knew I wanted my hair
short and had offered to cut it, but my mother wouldn't
let me. Beula was inspecting the short hairs on the back
of my neck with her cold, damp nose, sending nice little
shivers down my back. I liked the way Beula treated me
like one of the family.

"Your aunts visiting today, Jeannie?" Rose asked.
"Uh huh."

Rose laughed at my unenthusiastic response. "And
I bet your mom's cooking chicken in this heat." She lifted
her heavy hair away from her neck, exposing a navy,
white-ringed stained under the arm of her dress. She
smelled of sweat and Arid and face powder. "Either your
mom is a saint or else she's crazy, I can never decide
which."

The smell of browning chicken, sage and onions, was
beginning to drift over.

"A saint," Jake said.

Rose leaned back against Jake's bony knees. "Aw,
it's too darned hot to eat," she said. "You know, Jake,
what I'd like to be doing today? I'd like to be walking
in Stanley Park, with everything green and cool and people with umbrellas."

"Where's Stanley Park?" I asked, thinking we could maybe go there before supper.

"A long way from *here*," Jake said. I heard the scratch of a wooden match on the steps, and smelled the smoke of Jake's cigarette.

"It's in B.C., Jeannie, right by the ocean." Rose sighed and crossed her ankles. A ladybug that had been walking across her foot fell off into the dirt and lay there with its legs waving frantically in the air. I wondered if Ellen was still looking for the bedbug, and felt a little guilty, but not much. "It's so beautiful there, you just can't imagine, Jeannie. When I die, I'd rather go to Stanley Park than heaven."

Jake cackled. "Damn sight better chance of getting there, too." Rose didn't rise to the bait, I guess it was too hot. "Heaven never did appeal to me much," Jake went on. "All them gold sidewalks. Hard on the feet. Give me thick green grass any day."

"Yeah, you can say that again." Rose wriggled her toes as if she was feeling the springy green under her feet.

"Remember that little bridge in the park, Rose, where you can feed the swans?" Jake asked. "Jesus, them swans are big christers, Jeannie." I tried to imagine those big christers swimming around. Maryann laughed. Sometimes she was so quiet you forgot she was there.

"Yes, that's exactly what I'd like to be doing today. Feeding the swans in Stanley Park." Rose squinted her eyes and looked off into the distance, and you knew she was seeing all the way to Stanley Park, seeing the green and the rain.

"Maybe we'll go next year, Rose. Maryann sure

would love them swans. And the monkeys, eh? Crazy little buggers.''

"Wouldn't she, though? And it would be really something to look forward to, wouldn't it? We'll take Jeannie, too,'' she said, giving me an excited little hug. Rose was as good as her word, and in my mind I was already walking in Stanley Park, with the rain pattering on my new red umbrella.

Maryann had been listening intently, smiling till you thought her face would break. "Crazy little monkey buggers,'' she said. Beula clattered down the side of the steps, nearly stepping on Maryann who gave her a friendly swat on the rear as Beula went to suck up some water from her old tub. Then she trotted down to the end of the yard, scattering black pellets behind her, and settled down in the dirt beside the shed.

"And I just gave her a bath while you were at church,'' Jake said glumly. Beula looked at him and made an insolent sound in her throat.

Maryann finished her picture and handed it up to Jake, who looked at it carefully. I could see a purple, yellow-eyed panther peering back at him from behind a lacy blue tree.

"That's real pretty, sweetheart,'' he said, passing it down to Rose and me. "Isn't that pretty, now?''

"It's beautiful, honey,'' Rose said, and I agreed. It was, too, with the weird kind of beauty that all of her pictures had.

"Where's Beula?'' I asked. I couldn't see her anywhere in the picture, and she never drew one without Beula in it.

Maryann got up in that awkward way she had, pushing on the ground with her stubby fingers and sticking her legs out straight and stiff, her bum in the air. She pointed to a pair of eyes and part of one horn in the upper branches of the blue tree.

"Beula," she said. "There's Beula." Of course you could see it once you knew it was there, and we all laughed.

"It's like the pictures in that book of Maryann's, where you have to find a whole bunch of animals, all camouflaged," I said. It was the first time I'd ever used that word.

"Yeah, that's right," Rose agreed. "You sure fooled us, Maryann." She kept looking at the picture and smiling.

Maryann stood watching us, looking from one to the other, her round face all screwed up, small eyes intent, as if she could understand if she only looked hard enough. She put her hands on her stomach and giggled, eyes shut tight. "Fooled you," she said. It made you feel like hugging her.

"Ah, Rose, she's so good." Jake's voice behind us sounded strange. "She's so goodam *good*." He wrestled a handkerchief out of his pocket and blew his nose with a loud, honking noise that made Maryann laugh.

Rose reached over her shoulder and patted Jake's knee. She was still looking at the picture. "A purple panther," she said, "at least I think it's a panther," shaking her head and smiling. "Purple. You know, somehow you get to like those cockeyed colors."

"That's for sure you get to like them crazy colors."

Jake's voice was back to normal, and I looked at him then. He was squinting through the cigarette smoke, his eyes dark and shiny, the way they looked when he drifted down the street, singing, on Saturday night. ''Trouble is they start to make everything else look pretty damn dull.'' He was staring out at the yard, and turning back, I suddenly saw the old leaning shed, the bleached ochre weeds along the fence, the rusted washing machine he'd been meaning to fix for so long — Maryann had rolled her fingers into the wringer once — the pen he'd built when he brought Beula home, broken for ages now. Jake got up abruptly and went into the house, the screen door banging shut behind him.

Rose leaned over and butted the cigarette Jake had dropped beside the steps. She leaned back and sighed. ''Lord, it's hot,'' she said.

When I went home for supper, Maryann gave me the picture and I pinned it up on the wall at the foot of my bed.

After supper, I was sitting on the front steps with Tiger, our striped cat, when Jake came out of the house with his lunch bucket. He gave me a dark-toothed grin and a wave, and started off up the street, his narrow shoulders drooping inside his dark blue work shirt. A bald spot was beginning to show through the dark hair on the back of his head.

Long after the aunts had gone home, and Lloyd and my parents were asleep, I was still awake. My bedroom was like an oven, and I finally got up and went outside, soaking up the cool ground through the soles of my feet.

The moon was full, and Tiger was leaping around the garden, drunk on caragana again. On top of the Flodell's shed, Beula was asleep, her white coat ghostly in the moonlight. Everything in the yard was full of light and shadow, even the heavy tomatoes in the dark vines held the sheen of the moon on their smooth, round sides.

The Flodell's back gate creaked, and Beula gave a startled bleat. I expected to see Jake come up the path, and I had that tickly feeling in my stomach I'd get when I was planning to jump out and scare somebody, but it wasn't Jake, it was Mr. Wilson. He walked along the path and up the back steps and just stood there, with the moon on his white shirt and his shiny shoes.

Maybe Mrs. Wilson had died, people sometimes came for Rose at times like that. In the strange, white light, his freckles were bleached out, and his face looked naked, somehow, like Jake's had looked when we talked about Stanley Park. A moth flew around his head and bumped the screen. Then he knocked, and after awhile I heard someone moving in the kitchen, and the door opened with a soft little sighing sound. There was silence for a moment, then I heard Rose say, "Come in, Jim," her voice gentle, like when she talked to Maryann. Mr. Wilson went in and closed the door.

I lay awake for a long time that night, thinking about Jake and Rose and Maryann, and the Wilsons, and Ellen. Wondering if Mrs. Wilson had died; knowing she hadn't. Thinking about how people called her a good woman, about Jake calling Maryann good, how it wasn't the same. Realizing that *good* was the word I wanted at the railroad track when we were talking about Rose. Looking at Maryann's picture pinned on the wall, where the moon had faded it so it looked ordinary now. Wondering if I really liked Ellen after all. Wondering when I'd get to see Stanley Park.

EMILY

Every year we rented the same cottage at the west end of the lake. All through the dry, cold winter, when snow lay thick on the town, I dreamed about the lake; and in the summer, too, when parched prairie grass crackled under my feet and the caragana hedges were covered with dust. And still I was surprised, every year, by the shimmering immensity of it; you could barely make out the hills on the far side, and cottages were mere specks on the horizon.

On the first of July we were always up by six thirty to get an early start. That year my sister, who was fourteen, complained about getting up, but I didn't mind. In a corner of the back seat, made fort-like by a stack of pillows and blankets, I hugged my bathing suit and

imagined how it would be. The imagining was always
the same, made familiar by months of practise: I would
run along the warm wooden pier, dive into the cold water
and swim — just like that I would know how, my body
as easy and casual in the water as a fish's. Sometimes
I saved someone from drowning, most often my mother,
though how she was in danger of drowning when she
never went near the water I had never worked out
satisfactorily. She was always wearing a jersey print dress
and a straw hat, so I supposed she had fallen in.

But when we arrived and I raced into the water, I sank
like a stone. It didn't matter, it never mattered, the lake
itself was enough, the luxurious wetness of the water,
as clear as a crystal glass — no matter how deep you
walked in, you could always see the hard ribs of sand
on the bottom. I splashed in it, wallowed in it, soaked
it up through my pores, longing to pull off my tanksuit
but afraid my father or Val would catch me. I dogpad-
dled furiously, arms and legs churning foam, breath held
hurting in my chest, but when I stood up and looked
back, the stirred-up water extended only a few feet
behind me.

I was building a sand castle when Emily floated into
my life. A movement made me look up. She was floating
in the water about fifteen feet from shore, enormous
mounds of breasts and belly above the water, the back
of her head competely submerged, long hair drifting out
around her face like strings of brown weed. Just floating
there, without a sound, in that clear, still water. She passed silently by, parallel to the beach, and I shaded my
eyes to see her better.

She must be dead, drowned bodies rose to the top,
I knew that, and was just going to run for my father when
I saw her white foot move, just a flicker but still a movement, and farther on another, stronger flicker, like a
fish's tail, and she began to move faster. I watched her
for a long time, and then she rolled over and began to
swim. Until I saw her white arms gleaming rhythmically
in the sun I still half believed she was dead. I watched
for her all that day but she still hadn't appeared by
bedtime.

Ours was a plain two bedroom cottage with a screened verandah, its board siding weathered to a pale silver-
grey, soft and fuzzy to the touch, like suede. It was set
back in the trees, close enough to the lake to hear the
waves on a windy night, and fat spiders hung outside
the screens. The trees gave us the illusion of privacy,
though in fact we were close enough to our neighbors
to hear them talking at night, their screen door and toilet
door slapping open and shut, bursts of laughter. And
sometimes other sounds in the night. My father always
reserved the cottage on the day we left for the first of
July the following year. It gave us a proprietary feeling
and made it easier to leave.

Mr. Jacobson, the man who owned the cabins, called
renters ''summer people,'' which made us sound faintly glamorous. In fact we were quite ordinary, and this
didn't bother me yet but it bothered my sister consider-
ably. She had met some kids from the city last year, and
was afraid that we were going to shame her in some way,
do something horribly gauche or gross that she could
never live down. I swore I would never be a dumb snot
like her, but of course I was, a few years later.

It was almost dark when my father came in from fishing that first night and told us he'd had the scare of his life. He was fishing in the rowboat, a long way from shore, when a fat girl came floating by. He'd almost snagged her with his fish hook. It was downright spooky, he said, seeing someone that far out in the lake, just floating along as if she was ten feet from shore. He asked her if she wanted a ride but she didn't answer, didn't even lift her ears out of the water when she saw him speaking to her. She smiled and swam off, he said, and he followed her in to shallow water to make sure she didn't drown. She floated in and out of my dreams that night, a strange little smile on her lips.

"That's Dummy Morrow's daughter," Mr. Jacobson said the next morning in answer to my father's question, "your wife would know the family." Mother had grown up only a few miles from the lake. "Floats like a cork," he said, aiming a stream of tobacco juice into the long grass beside our cottage. A sturdy dandelion swayed, straightened, and dripped brown. "Emily, her name is, you'll get used to her. Swims like a fish and floats like a cork — swim clean across the lake if she takes the notion. And that ain't all." He didn't explain what he meant.

My mother had finished the dishes and was rolling cigarettes on the oilcloth-covered table when I went in. She was expecting company later and her hair was twisted onto hard metal curlers with rubber knobs. Because she had grown up near there she had a lot of company.

"Dummy Morrow," she said thoughtfully, lighting

a clumsy, hand-rolled cigarette, "I haven't thought of him for years." She blew smoke toward the ceiling while charred bits of paper and tobacco drifted onto her wine chenille robe. "In fact I thought they'd moved away." She absently scooped the loose tobacco into a pile on the table. Not many women smoked in those days, and Val had asked Mother not to smoke in front of her new friends, but she just laughed and went on lighting up whenever she felt like it.

"Did you know Emily?" I asked.

"No, I wouldn't know her. But I remember her father. He used to come around to the farm, sharpening knives and scissors and mower blades. He knew everything you said by watching your lips. And when he wanted to tell you something, he wrote a note."

"Was he deaf and dumb?"

"Of course," said my mother, "that's why he was called *Dummy* Morrow."

I accepted this without question or surprise, that was the way people talked then — Chinny Sawyer had a huge chin, Gimp Brown had one leg shorter than the other, Fat Faber weighed three hundred pounds. No one seemed to think anything of it, not even the Chinnys and Gimps and Fats, who waved and grinned when they were hailed by name.

"Do you think Emily is deaf and dumb?" Mother was putting things away in the bright blue cupboards on which someone had painted fat yellow fish with bubbles rising from their open mouths.

"She probably is," she said. "It's hereditary."

Emily was sitting on what I thought of as my stretch of beach when I got there. Even sitting, there was something of the same stillness about her, but she looked up and smiled as I went past her into the water. She was wearing a faded blue bathing suit and her wavy brown hair hung past her shoulders. Because of her size, I found it difficult to guess her age, she could have been thirteen or twenty. I attacked the water headlong, willing it to hold me up, but I could not keep my feet from touching bottom for more than a few seconds. Each time I glanced ashore, Emily was watching me intently.

And then she was in the water, gesturing for me to lie down, supporting me with her hand on the small of my back. I was stiff and awkward and she set me on my feet, shook her head and arms and legs and let them go limp, then she flopped back in the water and lay there. She put her hand on her chest so I would notice that she was breathing naturally. She was able to tell me with gestures what she wanted me to do, and I did it. There was authority in her manner, firmness in her hands, and before that first lesson was over, I trusted her completely. She smiled broadly when I managed to stay up for awhile without support, and then she signalled the end of the lesson.

While we were building an elaborate sand castle, my father walked down the dock with his green tackle box and fishing pole. I waved. "My Dad," I said, making sure Emily could see my lips. She smiled and nodded.

"Do you want to go fishing, Bethie?" he called, his voice sounding different across the water, distant, remote.

"No," I called back, "we're going swimming again."
I pointed to Emily and myself and made swimming motions with my arms.

He nodded and lifted his arm. "Be careful," he said,
and stepped down into the rowboat, almost losing his
balance before he sat down. As he rowed away, I promised myself I would go with him the next time he asked.

I don't know why, but we were not a family who did
many things together. I've heard it said that the Depression made families close, but it was not that way with
us. For one thing, there were four years between my
sister and me. There had been a baby who died two years
before I was born, a girl, too. She was beautiful, I'd
heard my mother say, with thick black hair and a perfect
little face. Her name was Elizabeth and they named me
for her; you'd think my mother would be afraid to do
that, afraid it would bring bad luck.

No, we didn't do that many things together. For that
matter, my parents didn't do many things together that
I remember. Certainly not at the lake, where my father
fished and my mother visited friends or read on the
screened verandah, drinking iced tea and fanning herself
with a cardboard fan with DRINK COCA COLA printed on it in red and white. She liked the stories in Liberty
magazine and saved them all up to bring to the lake.
She enjoyed the company she had there, too. She was
a woman who liked to talk and my father was a quiet
man; maybe it was years of poring over figures in the
small office in the back of the Co-op Store, maybe he
just got out of practise.

I discovered that first day that Emily was a fine person to build sand castles with. When we needed a flag for the turret, she raked the sand with her fingers and unearthed a small piece of silver paper, which she folded into a triangle. A quick raking on her other side produced a small twig which she split part way down with her strong fingernail, and sliding the paper into place, she poked it into the wet sand. She laughed when the wind caught it and turned it around. The sun was hot on my neck and arms, between my shoulder blades, and the warm wind fluttered and dried the wet sand on my legs.

Val came down to swim, walking in carefully, riffling the water with her fingers. In her white two-piece bathing suit, her blonde hair in a green net snood with small green bows on it, even I could see that she was pretty. "My sister," I told Emily, and she smiled and rolled her eyes in a complimentary way.

"Can I come with you?" I called. It was always better to ask, with Val.

"Sure. But don't splash me," she said, as I ran in. And I kept my distance, fearful she'd change her mind. I capered around her, telling her about the swimming lesson, telling her who Emily was, scarcely able to contain the huge bubble of joy in my stomach; I had to expand my chest to the limit to hold it. The sun, the lake, the absence of school, the swimming lesson, Emily, my sister . . . sometimes things were so good you could hardly stand it. I fell in the water face down and slowly sank to the bottom, my arms flung wide to take in the whole lake, the whole world.

Emily and I went in a half dozen more times that day,

and while she sat on the beach, I went on practising.
By the end of the day I could float on my back easily,
though I had to move my arms and legs more than Emily
did.

Once, while I was in the water, two boys came down
to the beach and seemed to be asking Emily to go
somewhere. She jumped up and ran off with them, her
long hair flying, joy in the pumping of her fat legs. They
disappeared into a clump of dense bush down the beach.
They were gone about twenty minutes and then Emily
was running back, looking over her shoulder and waving at the boys who didn't wave back, but who were giggling hysterically as they staggered off up the beach the
other way, shoving each other into the water every so
often, and they weren't even in bathing suits, they were
wearing pants and shirts and shoes.

I wonder if anyone else ever learned to swim as quickly
and easily as I did, for there could be no other teachers
like Emily. We were together every day, and almost as
easily as she had taught me to float, she taught me how
to breathe, how to move my arms and legs. I never wondered who had taught Emily, it seemed as if she must
have been born knowing how, as if her mother had
birthed her in the lake and she had swum easily from
one fluid to another. Sometimes, with motions for me
to stay close to shore, she would strike straight out toward
the centre of the lake until I couldn't see her for the reflec-
tion of the sun on the water. She always came back. And
every day we floated, side by side, wrapped in water,
the sun warm on our faces, open-beaked gulls hanging
in the blue air above us.

Val got a boyfriend, a boy from the city. I didn't like
him, though I couldn't have said why. He was polite
and good-looking but there was something about him
I didn't trust. They wound up the old Victrola gramaphone on the cottage verandah and danced to Bing
Crosby singing "Moonlight Bay" and "Sioux City
Sue." My mother grumbled about being relegated to
the back yard with her books and her visitors, but you
could tell she was pleased.

More boys came for Emily, they beckoned to her from
down the beach almost every day, and I soon accepted
these interruptions as part of our routine. I put in the
time while she was gone perfecting moats, straightening
flags — we had one on every turret, all different colors
— and squinting at the bushes now and then to see if
she was coming. If there were more boys, Emily was gone
longer. She always came back smiling, and sometimes
there were leaves in her hair.

Once her father came to the beach just as Emily and
two boys emerged from the trees. He was a thin, bald
man with thick glasses, and his hands moved so fast they
were almost a blur at times. I knew he was shouting at
her in his way. Emily's hands, which were slim and
graceful compared to the rest of her, moved more slowly
and there was no anger in her face. When he started pulling on her arm, she just shook him off, walked into the
water and swam away.

Emily was not there when we went back the next year.
She had been sent away to a special school for the deaf,
we were told.

I could make a collage of that summer with Emily if I had to, and I know exactly how I would do it. There would be the immense shimmering blue of the lake, and on the far shore, my father in the rowboat, fishing. My mother and another woman are in deck chairs, words falling out of their mouths into their laps; they are wearing dark glasses. Off to the left, my sister in her white two-piece bathing suit is dancing with her boyfriend and there are notes rising from the gramaphone. From a clump of bushes on the edge of the shore, boys' faces are grinning.

And right in the centre of that blue water, Emily and I are floating, floating in the silence like a strange pair of sea creatures. Emily's eyes, the color of the lake, are open, and her long hair is drifting out around her face.

THE TRITON

A woman sat on the dock watching, shading her eyes
from the glare of sun on water. About a hundred yards
out from shore, an empty blue boat drifted on the glittering lake, bobbing now and then on the swells from a distant power boat. The season ended early this far north,
the lake was almost deserted, except for the empty boat.

The woman stood up, thinking of calling someone,
when three men walked down the neighboring pier. Two
were policemen, their boots thudding dully on the wood.
A fat man in orange trunks jumped down into a boat
and began to unleash it from the pier. The two
R.C.M.P. stepped gingerly into the boat and sat primly
side by side in the bow as the fat man pulled on the rope
to start the motor. In their neat brown shirts and pants

and peaked caps they looked oddly out of place, like people overdressed for a party.

The motor didn't catch, and the man pulled the rope
again and again, his overflowing belly quivering with
the exertion. One of the policemen saw the woman.

"Did you see what happened out there, Ma'am?' He
pointed to the blue boat.

"No. I was just going to call someone when you came.
Has there been an accident?"

"It looks like it," he said, in a voice that might be
commenting on the weather. The water sucking against
the pilings of the dock made it difficult to hear. "We're
just going out to take a look," he added unnecessarily.
The motor caught with a sudden angry snarl, and the
boat leapt away from the dock. The empty boat rocked
gently, like a toy abandoned in the tub after the child
has been called to bed.

They reached their destination and cut the motor.
Their voices drifted over the water, quite clear in the
sudden stillness: "Incredible . . . sharp turn this way
. . ." the fat man swept his arm in a semicircle ". . .
fell out, just shot over the side." A deep voice, one of
the police, unintelligible, questioning. "No . . . no, happened so fast . . . don't think so . . . incredible," the
man said again, "gone just like that."

They stayed out for about fifteen minutes. The woman
stayed where she was, tensely watching and listening —
she couldn't imagine what clues they might be looking
for — and then they tied the blue boat behind theirs,
and began to tow it back to shore. Its bright paint glis-
tened in the sun as they chugged closer, and she made
out the name, THE TRITON, in neat white letters.

She looked past them at the lake, sparkling innocuously in the late afternoon sun. Somewhere under its surface was a man, alive an hour ago, now drifting and turning, his eyes open, his hair fanning out around his face. Pity, and something else, a kind of strange love for this poor thing in the water, gripped her hard and she looked away, surprised by the intensity of it.

Their voices intruded. ". . . coroner . . . call Hank about the . . ." ". . . doesn't matter now . . . stop and get some lunch." They had tied the boat to the dock and were preparing to leave.

"It's a drowning, all right." The one who'd spoken to her before called over, his young voice rather self-important, the way people sound sometimes when they are bearers of bad news. She nodded, her eyes inexplicably filling with tears. Water lapped the pier, slapped the large rocks at the water's edge, drowned out their voices as they walked up the neighbor's steps and disappeared from sight in the trees.

Then she heard them laugh. They had *laughed*. She looked at the empty boat, the empty water, bewildered by the men's laughter, by her own inappropriate reaction. She sat down again on the dock, hugging her brown legs inside her strong, sinewy arms. The lake was perfectly calm now, empty as far as she could see, its color deepening around the shore, where guardian pines were beginning to cast their shadows. Empty. Except for him. She stayed on the dock until very late.

Two boats began the search soon after the police left. The one belonging to the fat man, and another, larger boat. They cruised slowly back and forth, back and forth,

making wide, sweeping circles in the area, their voices
an occasional murmur above the muffled sound of the
motors. Now that the sun was almost gone, a damp chill
was closing in.

Still she sat. Anxiety tightened her stomach as she
strained to hear the men's voices. Don't laugh, she said
over and over in her head. Please don't laugh. Sometimes
whispering it aloud, like a fiercely protective mother with
a handicapped child exposed to the ignorance of
strangers.

The crest of each wave was tipped with orange sparks
from the setting sun when she rose stiffly to her feet and,
with a last, long look at the water, turned and climbed
the steep steps to the cabin. At the top of the stairs she
stopped and looked back. On the darkening water, the
wide path of the sun flickered and glowed. A gull bobbed
placidly through waves of fire, then suddenly rose on
the thrust of its strong wings, wheeled to the sun and
soared from sight.

*She could still see them. They walked as if there were weights
dragging at their legs, walked in slow formation toward the shore
— rows of men — hip deep, waist deep, knee deep in water,
like men landing at Dieppe. Their arms were held over their heads,
like soldiers surrendering, their hands lost in swirling fog. She
could not see their faces, did not want to see their faces, but kept
looking all the same, straining to see.*

Sweat slid from her armpits around to her back. The
dream flowed into reality with a vividness she had not
experienced since her childhood dream of a bear under
the bed. That recurring dream had been so real that she

would not tell her father when he came in answer to her cries, fearful he would look under the bed and be dragged in and eaten by the bear. So many years ago. But the bear, in one form or another, had been there always. Was there still.

She got up and went to the window, pulling back the green burlap curtain and searching the lake. In the smudged, ashen light of dawn it was grey, deserted. She let the curtain drop and felt her way back into the bed, just visible in the thick greenish grey light of the room.

This familiar cabin, her refuge through especially dark times, was hung with an assortment of things she took no notice of in the daytime, but which now, in the watery light, took on counterfeit life. The wooden wind chime became a squid, its tentacles hanging straight down; from the mobile by the open window a school of silver fish swam lazily; a paper Chinese lantern with silk tassels was a Portugese man-of-war. From somewhere on the dark lake came the clear, falsetto call of the loon. Ooo aaaaaaaah oo. Rising. Falling. A broken, pealing echo from another part of the lake. With a warm sense of peace, a rare thing, she floated into sleep.

She dreamed a shimmering underwater world. She dreamed a spiral shell. She dreamed a man. His eyes were luminous . . . blue-green . . . his hair lifting . . . drifting . . . he raised the spiral shell to his lips . . . Ooo aaaaaaaah oo.

She was at the dock early in the morning. More boats joined the search, including a police launch and another boat equipped with heavy chains. Once someone shouted excitedly and pulled an object to the surface, the massive chain clanking against the side of the boat. She didn't breathe until she heard him call out that it was a log.

She swam several times during the day, her strong arms propelling her through the water far past the point where she usually turned back because of her distaste for the long, clinging weeds. Once, as she floated effortlessly, she felt something touch her back, and then her thigh, gently brushing the skin.

Sometime in the afternoon, a neighbor, who was closing up her cabin for the season, came to the dock with mugs of coffee.

"They should find him by tomorrow," she said. "They usually bloat and rise to the surface in three days."

The woman didn't answer. She saw him surrounded with a soft, luminous aura, the dappled light flickering as he turned and turned in a slow, underwater ballet.

The neighbor shuddered. "You couldn't pay me to go in that water till they find him."

The woman's look was uncomprehending. "There's nothing to be afraid of," she said.

The neighbor, finding her not disposed to talk, took the cups and went away. Again night came and they had not found him.

She wakened early to the same thick, greenish light, another watery dream receding like a crab scuttling after the tide. Then she heard it, the sound that had taken her from the dream; a soft, bumping sound from the dock, as if something were nudging the posts. She got up, gathering the quilt around her naked body, and went outside.

The sound was louder there, and harsher — a boat, touching and scraping a pier as it rode the cold swells. She walked down the cold, dew-wet steps to the dock. Wrapping the quilt tightly around her in the damp dawn, she sat down to take up her vigil.

She should not have slept. She felt as if she had neglected a loved duty. Tonight she wouldn't sleep, she would stay there all night. She should have done that last night. What could she have been thinking of. She watched the far shore emerge from the mist, black pines a jagged line on the rosy horizon. Through the wisps of vapor that clung to the water, two black loons floated past, trailing V-shaped streamers of dawn. When the sun touched the water, she went back to the cabin to dress.

The search resumed, but yesterday's intensity had dissipated, as if they knew that the lake would soon yield what they sought. She swam again, the icy water taking away her breath at first, yet once she was accustomed to it, she felt she could go on forever. When she finally turned and looked at the tiny cabin, and the light dot that was the pier, it took a great effort of will to start back.

As she stood by the window, still in her swimsuit, the phone rang. Her son had had the phone installed, but she never used it. They would have heard of the drowning, would be deciding that she shouldn't be here alone. The ringing went on and on, as she looked out at the lake. She pressed damp footprints onto a sunny patch on the floor, watched them evaporate. Finally, after about fifteen rings, the phone was silent.

She lit the barbecue behind the cabin, still wearing

her bathing suit, with a warm jacket over it, not feeling the cold, though her legs were faintly blue under the tan. She sat in a deck chair, watching the coals begin to smolder. Red leaves spotted the grass under the trees, and she picked one up, rubbing its cool smoothness between her finger and thumb. The phone rang again. Rang and rang in the empty cabin, and she made no move to answer it. She squeezed the leaf in her fingers, distracted by the sound of the patrolling boats. She was not comfortable away from the water. Abruptly, the phone stopped ringing. Soon someone would come. A car would turn into the lake road.

Soft grey ash was forming on the rounded charcoal cubes, heat waves shimmered up, the trees undulating like underwater plants. The snarling sounds of the motors were muted, as if someone were cutting grass on a distant lawn.

In her haste she stumbled on the steps going down, grasped a tree trunk, righted herself. At the bottom step she dropped the heavy jacket, and on the stony shore she walked out of her sandals and into the water. The search boats were still a very long way off as she embraced the water and began to swim — rhythmically, purposefully pulling the numbing water past her body.

She swam out, out past the long, dark shadows of the pines, out where the sun touched the water. Where a warm sense of peace spread through her, as her strokes slowed and her limbs grew heavy.

BEHIND THE LINES

Rattle rattle rattle rattle BANG rattlerattle . . . The man next door was leaving home again. The clatter of his Supervalu cart on the sidewalk had wakened Merna.

She got up and peered down through the sheer bedroom curtains — sure enough, there he was going past under the streetlight, wearing the tan topcoat and brown hat he always wore when he left home. RattlerattleBANGrattlerattle — no wonder those carts didn't work worth a damn half the time, when people took them home and treated them like this. The cart was piled high with things; clothes stuffed into it every which way, a pantleg flapping over the side, a stereo speaker — she could only see one — a bag of golf clubs, she couldn't make out what else.

Fred wasn't in bed, he must have woke up with the racket and gone to the bathroom, or downstairs for something to eat. Or maybe he was already awake, he was going through another spell of insomnia lately. He'd blame it on the people next door, though; he'd been depressed about the neighborhood for quite awhile now, but it was hard to leave a house you'd lived in for twenty years. Fred was especially fed up with the man next door, but Merna found him entertaining in a weird kind of way.

He had stopped under the streetlight and was looking back at his house, at an upstairs window, by the direction of his gaze. He was a thin man with a long face that looked very pale under the light. Merna could faintly hear a woman's derisive voice, but couldn't make out what she was saying. She'd never seen her close up, the man's wife, or the woman he lived with, but she looked about a hundred pounds overweight and mean as a snake.

"Oh, no, you won't," he shouted up at the window. "You'll do no such thing." And when the disembodied voice droned on and on, the man next door went suddenly crazy.

He threw off his hat and shook his fist at the voice, he leapt up and down, screaming "nya nya nya blablablabla" in a mimicy voice, he jumped on his hat and kicked the cart, he shook his fist and danced around under the light like a fighter waiting for the bell, then he gave the finger to the house, waggling it around under the light so the woman wouldn't miss it, jammed his squashed hat on his head and went rattling off down the street. Merna felt like cheering.

74

RattlerattleBANGrattle, the sound grew fainter, and Merna climbed back into bed. Where did he go with that crazy grocery cart at three in the morning. And no wonder it sounded like it did, this had to be the third time she'd seen the man next door leave home. The rest of the time the cart reposed in their weedy front yard, or in a snowdrift by the back steps.

"Fred?" she called. Silence.

After a few minutes, Merna got up and went down the hall. There was a slice of light under the bathroom door. Clip clip clip clip, came faint, familiar sounds from the bathroom. Fred was clipping his moustache, a sure sign that he was disturbed about something. She didn't think the neighbors had anything to do with it; Fred was clipping his moustache a lot lately. There was no use asking him what it was, he wouldn't talk about it. A tom-cat yowled under the living room windows: All ryte? All ryte? All ryte? in a horrible, drawn-out Cockney accent. Cleo's furry feet hit the floor in the spare room and padded down the stairs. Merna went down and let her out so she wouldn't sit preening in the window while he prop-ositioned her all night long.

She'd just fallen asleep when Fred slid in between the covers. It was dawn. She opened one eye and saw him lying on his back, staring at the ceiling. His moustache was very, very neat. He sighed. After awhile, he carefully lifted his midsection and emitted a plaintive little fart.

The thought had crossed Merna's mind more than once that her life might be too good. She was grateful for it, of course, when she watched tv and saw people homeless from floods and fires and wars, read about middle-aged women taken in by pot-bellied polygamists. But nonetheless, she couldn't help noticing that the tenor of her days was just a little too even. Flat, one could almost say.

She had never had to fight for anything. Life had smiled on her the day she was born and kept right on smiling. She'd been a good daughter, obedient because she wanted to be; she was pretty — at forty-nine, she still was; and she had, in turn, raised good, obedient, handsome children. The seas of the last half of her life were as calm as the first because she'd had the good sense to marry wisely.

Many of the women she knew were not so fortunate. They had married men who turned out to be spend-thrifts, womanizers, alcoholics — one of them had even married a poet — and these men, charming though they were in some instances, had been found wanting in the long haul. So these poor women, and thousands more like them across the country, were having to carve out whole new lives for themselves: opening successful bou-tiques, having their paintings hung in shows that toured the provinces, dashing off with their briefcases to catch flights reserved for them by their secretaries. And when they were not doing these things, they were sitting over candlelit tables in swishy silk dresses with charming divorced men. The spendthrifts, womanizers, alcoholics. All reformed, of course.

While Merna, on whom fate had sprung no nasty sur-prises, sailed serenely into the sunset, her life as placid and unruffled as a stagnant slough. Lucky Merna. Mer-na had Fred, who was kind, industrious, honest, faithful, dull. Just a tiny bit dull, mind you, but then, so was she. So was their life.

She pondered all this as she sat in a deck chair in the sunshine, the morning after the man next door left home again. It was a gorgeous morning in late May, already hot at ten o'clock, the old apple trees in the yard heavy and fragrant with masses of pink buds. On the trunk of the elderberry tree, a grey woodpecker was pecking his little brains out. The picnic table under the elderberry was loaded with bedding plants, and Merna was looking forward to digging in the soil again. To getting her hands dirty.

Merna liked hard physical labor — the reason she jogged and worked out strenuously at a health club three times a week. She'd have made a good pioneer. Her great grandfather came west and homesteaded when he was seventy-five, and her grandfather and father had been country doctors. The family always proudly mentioned the great grandfather, but his little wife, four foot eleven in her high button shoes, had come with him.

Merna had no difficulty imagining herself, with children close to her skirts, helping to clear the land, build a log cabin. Or now. She was the kind of manager who could have fed good, nutritious meals to a big family on a shoe salesman's income. Sent them to university, too, and sat proudly at their graduations in a dress she'd sewn herself. Some of her friends were coping with aging, senile parents; Merna's parents were growing roses on Vancouver Island, walking miles every day and getting tanned on their sailboat in the summertime. To say nothing of what they were probably doing below deck.

So she did volunteer work, jogged, stripped wallpaper and painted walls before they needed it, all self-imposed challenges. All her life, Merna had been ready to rise to an occasion that never arose. She remembered her brother, Jack, who had stayed with them when his second marriage fell apart, she remembered him saying as he sat in their back yard soaking up whisky like a sponge, that "good old Fred needs to go to a foreign country and be shot at." Good old Fred was at that moment spraying the roses. Merna had known what Jack meant, people really did need to be shot at sometimes. Needed to dodge bullets, recover from wounds.

Actually, this morning Fred had had the look of a man who had been shot at, or was about to be.

"I hope that idiot next door stays away this time," he said sitting in the bedroom chair, putting new Odor Eaters in his shoes. "I feel like reporting him for disturbing the peace."

"Well, you can hardly do that." Merna was making the bed, pulling the heavy, quilted spread up over the queen-size pillows. "Are you sure you don't want some breakfast?"

Fred didn't answer. He was staring out the window, his profile, with his clipped moustache and short grey hair, looking rather sad and military — like a soldier surveying a field strewn with bodies. Or an officer looking ahead to a battle where there would be casualties. Fred was one of those men who looked more interesting in profile than front face.

She asked him again about breakfast.

"No, I'm not hungry." He sighed. "Connie can slip

out later and get me something from the muffin shop
if I need it." Connie was the new pharmacist he'd hired
when old Delbert finally hung up his pestle after fifty
years of dispensing drugs. Connie was a pale, Modigliani
kind of girl, with a long, thin neck that looked as if she'd
started to hang herself and changed her mind. She had
a personality like the old string mop they used to wipe
the dispensary floor at closing time.

"This neighborhood is getting worse all the time."
Fred pulled on his tweed jacket and stood looking out
the window. "Maybe it's just got too old, like the rest
of us."

"Speak for yourself," Merna said.

Fred was obsessed with age lately. Every night he added up the ages of the people in the obituary columns and
took the average. Actually sat there and figured out the
average, scribbling the figures in the margins of the
newspaper. When the average was in the seventies, or
sometimes in the eighties, he brightened, but when it
fell to the sixties, or, God forbid, the fifties, Fred looked
haunted. His best friend had died a year ago, collapsed
right in the middle of filling a prescription for Tagamet.
Fred was fifty-one.

"Well, you can joke about it if you want. This street
is going to the dogs and it's going to get worse." And
with this cheerful prognostication, Fred had gone off to
the store.

What Fred said was true. They'd bought this big old
house in the university area when the children were
small. Most of the neighbors were academics who never
raked their leaves, and who invited them to parties in

drafty, cavernous living rooms with fireplaces that
smoked, ancient carpets clawed to bits by cats, and stacks
of books and journals sliding messily over behind the
chairs. As the neighbors moved on to greener academic
pastures, some of the houses were bought for revenue
and chopped up into accommodations for students, who
partied noisily on weekends and chased each other
around in the long grass, rock music blaring as they
drank beer and washed their cars. Then there were the
people next door, who made the professors look, in
retrospect, like house-proud horticulturalists. And they,
at least, had the excuse that their minds were occupied
with higher things. God only knew what occupied the
minds of the people next door.

Merna got up and got the small gardening tools and
the spade from the garage, then hauled a huge bag of
peat moss out from the back porch. She took several
boxes of bedding plants from the picnic table over to the
side bed. The pansies had looked like a lost cause this
morning, flopped over the sides of the boxes with their
faces all collapsed in on themselves; but she'd watered
them anyway and they now looked as if they might actually live.

Merna was down on her knees, digging, when a door
slammed and the woman next door came out on her back
steps. Merna had a perfect view of her in an oval frame
formed by the communal hedge and a weeping birch in
the other yard. She wore a light, flowered wrapper and
red clogs. She yawned hugely, then clopped down a few
steps and sat down, pulling cigarettes from her wrapper pocket and lighting one, flipping the match out on-

to the lawn. She yawned hugely, and scratched herself under one breast, about the size and shape of a large vegetable marrow. She gazed out into the back yard, smiling slightly. The smile could only be described as anticipatory.

Merna looked around at all the work that needed doing in the yard. The grass would look even better for another good raking, both directions, with the snaggle-toothed rake. It was hellish hard work but it showed. This afternoon she wanted to finish the back flower beds, maybe get a few asters in along the side of the house, make a trip to the greenhouse for geraniums and lobelia for the patio boxes.

Then she remembered that Irene was coming for coffee. Irene and Jim were old neighbors who had moved to the suburbs, and Jim had left Irene for one of his graduate students last year. Irene was not one of the women Merna had been thinking of earlier. Irene was a casualty.

"That's easy for you to say, Merna, you have no idea," said Irene, gin and tonic in hand, thin, pale winter legs propped in the sun, "how humiliating it is to have someone call you up and tell you your husband is taking another woman on a trip, of course Nancy Thode couldn't wait to tell me, you know how she'd be enjoying it, the bitch, I didn't sleep a wink last night, and just when I was finally beginning to accept it, and he's taking her to Greece, Merna, to *Greece*, you know how I've always longed to go to Greece, and I couldn't get Jim to go anywhere, to Hawaii once and that was it and he hated every minute of it, he couldn't wait to get back to work, or that's what I thought then, I certainly know better now, and Nancy said . . .''

And on and on, with a face as long as a wet Sunday, her rings clicking like castinets on her thin fingers as she knocked back the drink she'd asked for instead of coffee. By the time she finished this speech, neither of them remembered what it was that was easy for Merna to say. Irene had a long face, with a furrowed forehead and corrugated frown lines between her eyebrows. She looked like a Bassett hound being taken to the vet. She also had an unfortunate whiny voice.

"Could we have another drink, Merna. God knows I need it today."

"How about coffee, Irene? You have to drive home and I have to start dinner soon. Besides, it will probably just make you feel worse in the end."

"Oh, God, Merna, now you're sounding like the rest of them. I can't stand it if you turn against me, Merna, everyone else is, even my kids, they hardly ever come and visit me, and it's easy for you to say I shouldn't be drinking, you have somebody to cook dinner for, I can't stand being the only woman in the neighborhood who doesn't have a husband to cook for — except for Lynn Holowaty and she has a lover, about half her age, they say, and speaking of Lynn Holowaty, did you know that she's making a mint writing Harlequin romances, they say she'll soon be making more than Bob, isn't that hilarious, and now the whole neighborhood is out barbecuing in their back yards again, I go in the house and pull the drapes when they start coming home, it's so goddam unfair, that's the part I can't stand, Merna, it's the *injustice*, when I think of Jim galloping around to Greece and God knows where all, splashing in the ocean with that, that fat *child* , that *Lolita*, and I'm left with the cat and the menopause, and if I died tonight in that big house all alone, that bloody cat would eat me, and you tell me not to drink, I look in the mirror and see the world's oldest living woman . . .''

When Irene finally left, Merna put two potatoes in the oven, seasoned two steaks and tossed a salad. She was out in the yard, planning where to put the rest of the bedding plants, when the phone rang.

"I'm sorry, Merna, I'll be late for dinner. I'm having a drink with someone."

Something told Merna not to ask with whom. "Oh. That's fine. How late do you think you'll be?"

"I'm not sure. And Merna? Can we talk when I get home?"

"Of course," said Merna, over the little alarm bells that were going off all over the place. "I'll be here."

And she was. She was still there when he had come and gone with his two navy Samsonite bags. It had been such a civilized discussion. He just needed some time to himself, to make some decisions, he'd been wondering lately if he didn't need a major change in his life. No, he didn't know what kind of change, he just wasn't sure any more that he wanted to spend the rest of his life filling prescriptions and . . . and coming home to her, he meant, but didn't say so . . . no, there was no other woman . . . she was being wonderful about this, he would call in a few days, he didn't think he'd even go into the store, he just wanted to think, and then he was gone, leaving behind an almost empty closet, except for a discarded Odor Eater, curling at the edges, like a dried-out paramecium.

Merna cried when he left. It was a terrible shock, though she should have been expecting it, must have been blind not to see it coming. It was all there: his wandering around the house at night, clipping his moustache, his obsession with the obituaries, dragging Connie's name into the conversation somehow every day, infatuation did that to people. Even his polite little interrogatory farts, heard faintly from behind the bathroom door each morning, had sounded especially wistful lately. Am I really fifty-one? they asked. Is this all there is?

She blew her nose and made a pot of coffee — real, perked coffee that cheered her up a little. She took a cup outside with her, trying to decide what to do until dark. Amazingly, there was still enough time to put in a few more plants, better than sitting feeling sorry for herself.

She looked at the plants she'd put in this morning. This morning, when she was still Lucky Merna, with a husband to cook for. The plants were looking wonderful, right at home, as if they hadn't been pitched out of their familiar bedding boxes just a few hours ago. A branch that grew too low on the apple tree snagged her sweatshirt as she went past and she got the saw and sawed it off. Then she dragged it out in the alley and sawed it up in pieces, and painted the trunk with some preparation she found in the garage. She was actually enjoying herself. Shock, no doubt. People acted strange at times like this.

Fred must think she was an idiot, saying there was no other woman. He was with that noodle-necked pharmacist. Proximity, that's all it was. At the first symptom of discontent, she had whipped out the prescription, and was probably this moment filling it.

Merna eyed the elderberry tree by the back steps. It needed a thorough pruning to get out all the old dead stuff. That woodpecker this morning had known something they didn't, it was probably full of termites or something. She got the pruning tool, climbed up on the picnic table, and started on the lower branches.

What Fred could see in that limp young woman was beyond her. What would she be, about twenty-three or twenty-four? Slightly protruding eyes, too, maybe she had a goiter, God knows they'd probably come back with everybody going off salt. As Merna pruned each dead branch, she dragged it out from the tangle of new growth and other dead wood and threw it on the lawn. Soon she had a great, towering, twiggy pile. All she needed was a witch. She'd finish this job tomorrow, get at the lawn, really work up a sweat, go for a long run.

She mustn't underestimate the attraction that girl had for Fred. The very fact that she wasn't pretty was probably a bad sign, made it more serious, and she did, after all, have youth on her side. "I look in the mirror and see the oldest living woman," she heard Irene saying.

She jumped down off the picnic table, ran upstairs to the full length mirror in the guest room, and peeled off her clothes, scattering leaves and bits of twigs on the

floor. She peered at herself. She went and got her glasses
and had a better look — it was ages since she'd really
looked at herself. She looked damned good for forty-nine.
Damned good for any age. Her breasts were especially
nice, but then they were only thirty-eight. She was firm
and trim, and still quite brown from their yearly trip
to Phoenix — she was dark-skinned and held her tan
long after Fred's had disappeared. Maybe he was planning to take Connie to Phoenix next year — she could
use some sun, that pale string, she looked like the devil
in white. But what gave her the idea that she could go
to Phoenix or anywhere else with Merna's husband,
that's what she'd like to know. They were probably planning to go to somewhere interesting. Like Greece. Merna
got dressed and went back outside.

She pruned as much of the tree as possible without
a tall ladder, and decided to leave the rest. It was starting to get dark anyway. She walked around, absent-
mindedly planning what plants to place where, and
breathing in the spicy scent of petunias. The pansies,
that had languished in their boxes, now stood at attention, bristling with greenery, their big, expectant faces
wide open.

Rattle rattle rattlerattleBANGrattleBANGBANGrattle
. . . The man next door was coming back down the
street. As he came closer, the front door of his house
smacked open, and the big woman stepped out and stood
with her hands on her hips. She was still wearing the
flowered wrapper and red clogs, and her jaw would
deflect bullets.

She waited. Like a panzer tank waiting for a, well,

a grocery cart. BANGrattleBANGBANG . . . they were going to need a new cart soon if this kept up. As the man next door drew opposite Merna, who was pretending to look at the flower beds along the walk, he lifted his hat politely.

"Lovely evening," said the man next door, who probably wasn't going to be the man next door for long.

"Yes, lovely, isn't it?"

The pantleg was now tucked into the cart, and a jacket sleeve hung forlornly over the side. On the shelf under the cart lay an enormous box of Black Velvet chocolates with a red bow on it.

The woman next door was walking down their driveway with a slow, measured tread. A massive arm came up, rotated slightly, like a gun in a turret, and followed the man till he was opposite her. One fat finger pointed between his eyes.

"Keep going. Just keep moving, and don't come back."

He had slowed down, but now speeded up, with an embarrassed glance at Merna over his shoulder. He was almost past the house.

"Hold it!"

He stopped. Looked hopeful.

The woman walked across the lawn to the cart, reached down and extricated the box of chocolates, hugging them to her fat bosom.

"Now, march!"

And he rattled off down the street, while the woman went back across the weedy lawn and into the house, slamming the door.

Well. Well. It just wouldn't be the same without the man next door.

Merna put all the tools in the garage, and then she decided to make another pot of coffee. She needed to draw up some plans, some kind of campaign. No simp of a girl was going to steal her husband and run off to Greece with him, while she stayed home with the cat. And even if Fred never came back she wouldn't be caught dead in Irene's great battalion of wronged women.

No. She'd start by getting the place ship shape for summer, and then fly to the east coast to see Ellen, her old university friend, who had, thank you very much, had a very good life since the late sixties, when Lawrence had run off with some girl covered in hair and beads, and had a baby with her. That child must be a teenager, now. Merna still remembered how shocked they'd all been — Ellen and Lawrence were the first. And they were a generation that remembered Ingrid Bergman and Roberto Rossellini, for God's sake.

Ellen had been asking her for years to come and see the craft shop that had paid the bills for her and the kids — to see the east coast, meet Ellen's friends. She'd call tonight. Tell her she was coming. It was a good idea to stick with the survivors, like Ellen. Besides, Merna had often thought of opening a shop of some kind, and Ellen could give her lots of pointers. She'd give Lynn Holowaty a ring, too. She hadn't seen Lynn for ages.

And as soon as she got back from Ellen's, she'd go to Vancouver to visit Jack, who was still being shot at. It would be great to see her brother again. And Ellen. Fred wasn't the only one who needed a change.

She carried her coffee upstairs, checked her closet to see what she needed to buy for travelling. Going away was probably a very good tactic, anyway, it would give Fred something to think about. Besides, there'd be gossip, and she didn't want sympathy. Or need it. She was feeling quite happy and excited, no doubt she was still in shock.

From the halls of Montezuma . . . To the shores of Tripoli . . . she hummed as she started making lists of things to do and buy before she left.

The phone rang. Who would that be at this hour? Probably one of the kids. Should she answer it? Yes, she couldn't stand not to, but she wouldn't say anything yet about Fred, just pretend he was in bed if it was for him.

We will fight the nation's battles . . . On the shores and on the . . . she whistled, as she ran lightly down the stairs.

"Hello?"

"Merna? Is that you?"

"Yes, it's me. *Fred?*"

"You sounded so happy, I thought maybe I had the wrong number."

"Oh." Was she supposed to say she was sorry? "Well. I'm all right, I guess." Silence. "How are you?"

"Merna, I can't sleep." He sounded plaintive. As if it was somehow her fault. Likely Connie didn't sleep with a slab of plywood under her mattress. Really, this was too much. She imagined Connie there beside him, and it hurt, but less than she might have imagined. What she felt was anger. And embarrassment. Fred should know better.

"I just can't sleep in a strange bed," Fred was saying. She was having difficulty taking this in.

89

"Fred, where is Connie?"

"Who?"

"You know who. Connie."

There was a little silence, and Merna could hear Fred's snuffly breathing. His allergies were acting up again.

"Do you mean Connie from the store, Merna? How would I know where she is. With her boyfriend, most likely. What's she got to do with anything?"

No Connie? No affair? Merna's heart sort of jumped up and keeled over, all in one motion.

"Fred . . . where are you?"

"At the Sheraton, but I think I'll come home."

"*Tonight*? You're coming home tonight? You haven't had time to make any big decisions, have you?"

"Yes, I have. All I need is a holiday. How would you like to go to Phoenix for a couple of weeks? Delbert would come in and help Connie look after things. That's all I need, Merna. That, and a good night's sleep."

"But you've paid for the room and everything. Why not stay until tomorrow?"

"I want to sleep in my own bed, Merna." There was a long, sniffly silence. She could hear the tv news faintly in the background.

"You're acting very strange, Merna. Almost as if you didn't want me to come home."

Merna sighed.

"Don't be silly, Fred. Come on home."

IN THE VALLEY OF THE KINGS

She was carrying a basket full of dirty clothes down
to the laundry room the first time she noticed the smell.
She stopped in the front hall and sniffed. Something
dead. A mouse, she thought, crawled into the register
and died — surely the caretaker couldn't ignore that,
as he did everything else around the place.

Awkwardly she pushed open the door leading to the
downstairs apartments and manoeuvered the laundry
basket through, trying not to breathe too deeply. Now
that she thought of it, a faint odor of decay perpetually
hung in the halls — ancient dust, musty stains in the
beige carpet, dry, recycled air, sometimes overlaid but
never obliterated by the pungent smell of disinfectant.

In the small, overheated laundry room she sorted the

washing into two small loads, wishing she had a different day on the laundry schedule. Monday nights the Auditorium showed travel films. It was something to do, somewhere a woman could go alone and not look out of place. Lots of *old* women went to the travel films alone, but old women, alone and in twos or threes, never looked out of place. You expected it. Were almost surprised when you saw one with an old man. She saw such worlds of living in their faded eyes: births, deaths, grandchildren, turkey dinners. Tonight the film was The Valley of the Kings, taking you right inside those ancient tombs where mummies had taken forever to disintegrate under wide-eyed funerary masks. They were surrounded by jewelry, statues, paintings, even bowls of pigeon stew, the man said last week, and the two old ladies beside Alice had laughed and said now they knew the pigeons on their building were good for something. Sometimes Alice went anyway on Monday night, but then she ran out of clean clothes before the end of the week and had to wash things out by hand, cluttering her tiny bathroom with their drying.

Her laundry was more work than it should have been for someone living alone. She perspired nervously, copiously, at times, and synthetic fibers announced the fact to everyone in the office. Six cotton blouses, five of them white, all tailored with long sleeves. She put the white blouses in the washer and sprinkled Bold on them. Her sheets and towels, which looked as if they hadn't been used since last washday went into the other washer.

A record player was thumping away when she reached the first floor. The girls across the hall had company

again. She heard male voices and laughter as she un-
locked her door with the key she carried on an elastic
around her wrist since the time she'd forgotten it and
had to get the caretaker to let her in. There was a sudden burst of delighted laughter from number ten and
she closed the door quickly behind her, but she could
still hear it. In the bathroom she washed her hands with
water as hot as she could stand. The caretaker would
have to find whatever had hidden away and died.

The apartment block was cheaply built and she often
heard the couple who lived above her moving around,
heard their toilet flush, heard them when they made love,
which was often. She put a pillow over her ears then,
holding her body still in bed until the rhythmic sounds
overhead had stopped. Sometimes, from her bathroom,
she could even hear the trickle of their peeing. She should
move out of here to someplace better, she could afford
it, but somehow it didn't seem worth the effort. Nothing
would change. It never did. She'd buy some earplugs
tomorrow, she'd been meaning to for months.

She washed her hair and rolled it on plastic curlers,
detesting, as always, its limp mousiness. Darlene, from
the office, had suggested she have it colored and get a
curly perm, an idea that intrigued and alarmed her, but
she'd never done it because of her mother. Women who
dyed their hair were forever equated in her mother's
mind with the woman who had run off with Alice's
father. Alice was five when he left.

She had one very vivid recollection of her father,
laughing and laughing, his teeth very white against his
dark skin, as he tried to kick the lightbulb that hung down

from the kitchen ceiling. She had tried to imitate him, she'd been wearing a red dress and black patent shoes with straps across the insteps, and it seemed a marvelously funny thing they were doing together, laughing and kicking, with the light winking on the toes of her shiny shoes.

Then he'd picked her up and danced her all around the kitchen, his rough, warm cheek held tight against hers, singing "In my sweet LIttle ALice red gown, I lala wander DOWN into town . . (laugh, swoop, hold on tight) . . la la both PROUD and shy . . (so warm) . . as I felt EVery eye . . (so high) . . and in EVery shop winDOW (swoop, giggle) . . I'd primp PASSing by . ."

Oh, she'd felt so pretty, so *special*, as they whirled and swooped around and around the kitchen, Alice's arm tight around his brown neck, reaching for the lightbulb with her other hand whenever they came close to it, always just missing it as he swooped her away, both of them laughing and laughing.

And then there was her mother, tightlipped and pale, in the kitchen doorway, and that was the end of that. One morning, when Alice got up, he was gone and she never saw him again, but she never forgot that night — his rough, warm voice, the dancing and the laughter. And she hadn't known until years later that he'd changed the words of the song to match her dress.

She finished her hair, the bright yellow rollers accentuating the pallidness of her skin. Like her mother's, she thought, staring listlessly in the mirror. Someday she would become another pale beige woman; hair, skin, eyes, even her teeth, the same mean shade of beige. The stereo and laughter across the hall were getting louder: "For there's still a lot of wine and lonely girls," sang a deep, male voice accompanied by a guitar, "In this best of all possible worlds."

Alice turned on her radio to drown it out, and sat down at the table in the small dining alcove to write to her mother. She took her mother's last letter from its black shoe box and read: *It's nice that Brian is coming to dinner with you Sunday, he sounds like such a nice young man. He doesn't drink, does he? You know you can't trust a man who* . . . Oh, yes, that's what she had told her last. She always had to check before writing because there wasn't any Brian, she'd made him up, as a gift to her mother. It wasn't her mother's fault that there were no Brians in her life. That there never had been.

Alice picked up the pen and wrote on the pale green stationery: *Dear Mother. Good news. Brian got a promotion to head teller at the bank. He's taking me out to dinner to celebrate on Saturday night, and then to the Royal Winnipeg Ballet.* She looked up, tapping her teeth with the pen, trying not to see the red devil faces on the hideous flocked wallpaper beside the table. She'd lived with the paper for six months without seeing the faces, and now she couldn't not see them, they leapt leering out at her the moment she looked at the wall. She really should move, this place was getting on her nerves. The people who passed her in the halls as if she were invisible, the rows of shabby mailboxes in the front entry, hers always empty except for her mother's weekly letter and the utility bills.

Darlene is going shopping with me tomorrow to help me pick out a new dress for Saturday night, she wrote. *I saw a nice one in the Midtown Plaza the other day, a lovely shade of blue and not too expensive. Don't worry, Mother, Brian doesn't drink, he says that's not the way to get ahead.* She looked at her watch, the blouses would be finished.

She came back from putting them in the dryer and scrubbed her hands thoroughly to remove the faint odor of decay they had picked up downstairs. She examined a black skirt that hung neatly in her closet beside the grey, navy and brown skirts. It would do for work tomorrow, and Tuesday nights she sponged and pressed them all. Her hair was nearly dry, would be by the time she finished the letter and went to bed. She felt very tired. She always did.

As she prepared her breakfast the next morning — one poached egg on whole wheat toast — Alice realized that the awful odor had crept into her apartment overnight, seeped in under the door while she slept, like some obscene exhalation. There was no excuse for it, that caretaker must be aware of it, even with the whisky fumes that hung over him like a cloud. She hoped she wouldn't have to speak to him about it, he disturbed her with his shrewd little eyes that seemed to be saying he knew something about you you didn't know yourself. Something you wouldn't want to know. Sometimes she heard him joking and laughing with the girls across the hall, but when he saw Alice, his little, knowing eyes flicked away.

It was another frigid morning, with the city shrouded in a heavy ice fog, and the bus was late. The office clock showed twelve minutes after nine when she'd hung her coat in the women's washroom and sat down at her desk. She'd run all the way from the bus and now realized, with a tightening in her stomach, that the cold, clammy perspiration that had started on the bus when she knew she'd be late for work had soaked through the underarms of her blouse. Her hands were like ice, and the cold in her feet was creeping up her legs. She really should see a doctor about the cold hands and feet. When she had to shake hands with someone, which wasn't often, she always mumbled some excuse for her cold hands. The only time the excuse had any validity was when she'd been holding a cold drink.

The next desk was empty. Darlene was late, too. But she would breeze in, exuding good spirits and Charlie perfume, with some long, involved story about why she was late. Once she'd told them a man had shot at the bus with a rifle, she'd had the entire place spellbound with that one. Alice hadn't believed her until she'd heard it on the news that night. Darlene lived a life full of high drama, or so she made out, but then she could build the most trival thing into a story that even amused or impressed Mr. Derkop.

Alice felt Mr. Derkop looking at her from his glass cubicle. He was a large, bald man with small eyes, and she thought of him sometimes as an octopus in an aquarium, could picture his waving tentacles hidden by the lower wooden section of his office. Les, the junior accountant, had his desk in one of those half-glass offices, too, but she never thought of him that way. Les was nice. A friendly, warm person. Darlene had designs on him, she knew, and Alice hoped he would have more

sense than to fall for Darlene. Les was hard at work
already, his blonde head bent over his desk, as she took
the stack of invoices from her In basket. She would take
her coffee break at her desk to make up for the twelve
minutes. She was exhausted and the day had just begun.
She'd go to bed right after dinner tonight.

At 5:30, when she opened the heavy apartment door,
the stench hit her like a kick in the stomach. The mid-
February sun, which had come out about noon, had been
pouring in the large front windows and the front hall
was stifling hot. Alice clamped a gloved hand over her
nose and mouth, not breathing till she was inside her
apartment. Even her coat smelled of it as she hung it
in the closet. Then she scrubbed and scrubbed her hands,
scouring the skin and nails with a nailbrush, and still
she wasn't satisfied that it was gone.

There was no need for anyone to tell the caretaker
now, the whole building must know. It was definitely
not a dead mouse. It was more like the freezer full of
spoiled meat she had smelled once, gone bad while the
people were away on holidays, come unplugged or something. Perhaps it was a body, you read about things like
that sometimes. Like the story she'd read just last week
about the woman somewhere in the States who died at
home, and when the neighbors finally called the police,
they found the woman's father, or what was left of him,
in an upstairs bedroom. He'd been dead for seven years.

Well, thank goodness she didn't have to go through
the hall again until morning. There was a letter in her
mailbox, she'd seen it from the corner of her eye as she
rushed past, but it would be from her mother and could

wait. It wasn't time yet for the light bill and she'd had the phone taken out months ago, glad to be rid of its squat black presence.

The next morning at coffee time she told the others about it. There was a small alcove at the back of the office, with two tables, a cupboard and sink. The shiny brown mugs had red metal strips attached, with their names in raised white letters, as if they might be in danger of forgetting who they were, or who the others were. Darlene had labelled the cups one day when she wasn't busy.

The others were already gathered when Alice came back from scrubbing her hands; the awful odor clung to her, she was sure, especially when she perspired. She poured coffee and sat down with Mrs. Hayes, Mr. Derkop's secretary.

"There's something dead in my apartment building," she blurted out.

Les, who was nursing a too-full cup of coffee to the table, looked startled. "Really?" He pulled a chair up to the table. "How do you know?" Mr. Derkop and Darlene, at the other table, stopped talking and stared over at Alice.

"Because of the terrible smell in the halls," Alice said.

"Something dead?" cried Darlene, her eyes lighting up. "There are quite a few dead ones in my building, too, but they don't smell yet."

"Oh, God." Les looked pained, but then he smiled. He was too kind to hurt anyone.

"Darlene, you're awful," said Mrs. Hayes, lighting

one of those thin brown cigarettes she smoked. Embarrassment ground at Alice's stomach. Why had she said that about the smell? It sounded vulgar. Like something Darlene would say.

"Is it in one particular place, or all over the building?" Mrs. Hayes was looking at her sympathetically. People on buses and in cafeterias poured out their life stories to Mrs. Hayes, and Alice could see why.

"In the front hall, mostly. It's all over, really, but stronger there. It's so bad it burns your nostrils," Alice heard her own voice going on; realized, with some surprise, that they were all listening. "At first I thought it must be a mouse that got into the register and couldn't get out."

"It doesn't sound like a dead mouse," said Mr. Derkop. Mrs. Hayes nodded meaningfully.

"A cat or dog, maybe?" Les suggested. "Come in out of the cold and got locked in somewhere."

"It could be," Alice agreed. "That's probably it." The tone of her voice saying, No, not that. Something worse.

"I bet it's a body," Darlene chimed in. "You hear about things like that all the time, people dying alone and nobody knowing." Her eyes sparkled as if she were about to tell them a joke. "Did you read that story in the paper a week or so ago about that woman in California? The one with the dead father upstairs?"

"Oh, trust you to think of that," Mrs. Hayes said, but her smile was loving. They all laughed, Darlene loudest of all, and she winked at Les as if the two of them found Mrs. Hayes in some way peculiar and boring, the kind of person who might die with nobody knowing.

"I really think it may be a . . . ." Alice hesitated, "a
. . . you know . . . that." She finished lamely and looked
down at her hands in her lap. The fingernails had a faintly bluish cast.

"God, what an awful thing." Les was looking at Alice
with real concern. "Why doesn't somebody do something?"

"Well, maybe they're looking. I'm not sure they're
not."

"Just don't let it get to you. They'll have to clear it
up soon." Les got up and shoved his chair in, dropping
his hand to Alice's shoulder for a moment, giving it a
little squeeze. "Keep us posted."

"Oh, they'll have to," echoed Mrs. Hayes, butting
her cigarette. "Lord, yes."

Les went out, muttering something about how much
he had to get done before lunch, and Darlene groaned.
"Yeccch! Me too, I guess. No rest for the wicked." She
gave an exaggerated sigh as she stood up. "Alice, if you
want to spend the night at my place, let me know. Being
around somebody dead is enough to give anybody the
creeps."

"Oh. Well, thanks, Darlene. That's nice of you, but
of course I don't know for certain that it's that."

"Suit yourself."

Darlene began twitching everything into place: volum-
inous bloue, skirt, vest, silver chains, high-heeled sandals. She fluffed up her curly hair and applied plum-
colored lipstick, using the electric kettle for a mirror, happily oblivious of her fascinated audience of three. Her
long nails were the exact same shade of plum.

"Don't forget, Alice. I've got a couch I can pull out. Just phone first if you're coming." She stopped on her way out and winked over her shoulder. "In case I've got a gorgeous man hidden under my bed." And went out laughing.

Mr. Derkop shook his head and smiled. "That girl," he said, ruefully. "That girl," he said again.

Mrs. Hayes and Mr. Derkop got onto the weather, their favorite topic, and Alice sipped her lukewarm coffee. She normally took only ten minutes for coffee, but she felt like taking a little extra time for once, having another cup of coffee. Everyone else did now and then.

She wouldn't go and stay with Darlene, of course, she'd be too uncomfortable getting ready for bed in someone else's place, but she had been asked. She had been asked. She would write and tell her mother. Alice ran her thumb back and forth over the metal tag on her cup and took a happy little sip of coffee.

Back at the apartment after work the problem had worsened. Her coat breathed foully as she hung it on the shower rod and turned on the fan. Then she scrubbed and scrubbed her hands, using a bit of Comet to brush under the nails, which needed cutting again. How Darlene could type with those long nails, claws almost, was a mystery. She let the warm water run on her hands to warm them up, till the nails lost their bluish color.

She really should move to a warmer climate, the coast maybe, but she didn't know a single person there, and today in the office, it was almost as if she belonged, the warm feeling in the little coffee room. And of course there

102

was her mother. If she moved, she would have to take her mother. Alice had a sudden vision of herself and her mother in some lush, green landscape; two pale, narrow women in good black coats, twin spectres drifting through the mist. She shivered and turned the water off. The couple upstairs were chasing each other again, muffled shrieks, thumps and laughter echoed down the air vent in the ceiling. She went out and closed the bathroom door behind her. Tomorrow on her lunch break she would buy the earplugs.

"Have they found it yet?" Darlene asked avidly as Alice sat down at her desk the next morning. "Have they found out who died in the building?"

"No, not yet, if that's what it is. But they're finally going to do something about it. I heard the caretaker telling one of the tenants when I left."

"What's to do, for God's sake? All they need to do is follow their noses."

"I know. I heard him say the manager of the building was coming this afternoon. He doesn't want the responsibility, I guess. The caretaker, I mean."

Darlene ripped a page from her typewriter and rolled in a fresh one. "He sounds like a real winner, that man," she said. And the clatter of her machine ended the conversation. Darlene assaulted the typewriter the same way she attacked everything in life: noisily, erratically. But somehow cheerfully.

"Don't forget," she called, over the racket. "Call me if you want to stay over at my place. I could come and pick you up."

Of course Darlene would like to be in on the excitement, but this didn't annoy Alice as it would have once. She liked the offhand way Darlene had dispatched the caretaker, taken away his power. *"He sounds like a real winner, that man,"* Alice said to herself, and smiled.

The body in the building dominated the coffee time conversation, all of them fascinated by it. Surrounded by their smiles, questions, surmises, commiserations, Alice felt warmth spreading tentatively through her body, felt her neck muscles relaxing. Even her hands and feet were warm. Strange that something so morbid had given rise to this feeling of cameraderie and, with all of them talking at once, a kind of frenetic joy, almost. As if they were celebrating something.

"Brrrrr," Mrs. Hayes said, finally, with a mock shudder. "Let's talk about something cheerful. Like the staff party."

They attacked the subject of the staff party on Valentine's Day with the same verve, all of them overstaying the usual fifteen minutes. Alice *must* go to the party, they all agreed, she needed to get out of that depressing place and have some fun. They were going to The Embers, where the food and music were wonderful. They teased Mr. Derkop, deciding to all have steak and lobster and the most expensive drinks on the menu, and he didn't seen to mind, seemed, in fact, to like it. Alice heard herself laughing out loud. She forgot for awhile about the faint, repulsive odor which she was sure, had insinuated itself into her skin, clothes, hair. She even forgot to be embarrassed about her hands, rough and red from the frequent scrubbings. But she knew, of course, that it was still there, and back at her desk she made a mental note to buy some Lysol at the drugstore to put in her shampoo and bath water.

On the way home on the bus, Alice balanced the parcels on her lap — small packages from the drugstore, the Bay, and a large dress box from a shop called The Jungle. She'd seen the dress in the window at noon hour — gauzy, shimmery, a rosy shade of red, the most beautiful dress she'd ever seen, and here it was in a box on her lap. She'd asked the clerk if she could return it in case she changed her mind about going to the party. But why would you want to do that, the clerk had asked, sounding genuinely puzzled, it does wonders for you.

And it did. It really did. The color flushed her cheeks and her eyes had shone with excitement as she looked in the mirror. In a dress like that there were suddenly possibilities. She would flicker like a warm flame. Les might even ask her to dance. She just needed to wear a touch more makeup with the dress, the clerk had said kindly as Alice made out the cheque with trembling hands.

The February thaw was continuing and some of the passengers on the bus had lost the closed, stoical look they'd assumed as winter went on and on. They looked tentatively hopeful, as if they might begin to believe in spring again. Alice remembered Les's hand on her shoulder, its warmth filtering through her blouse to the cool skin beneath.

At the front door of the apartment building, she fumbled for her key. Through the glass she saw several people standing around: the caretaker, the two girls from across the hall in blue jeans, some other tenants, a man in a dark suit. She almost dropped her parcels as she struggled to extract her key from the lock and pull open the heavy door. No one offered to help. She went past them up the stairs, holding her breath against the hot, putrescent air that burned her eyes and nostrils, hung like a pall over the people in the entry.

Inside, she put the dress box on her bed and put the bag of disinfectants under the bathroom sink. Then, after washing her hands thoroughly, she unpacked the bag from the Bay, lining up its contents on the white countertop. A bottle of rosy foundation, deep rose blusher, eyeliner, mascara, a neat plastic case with four jewel-like shades of eyeshadow, lipstick in a shiny silver case. Suddenly the small, utilitarian bathroom took on a festive air.

In the bedroom, she opened the box and carefully lifted the dress from its tissue-paper nest. The nice clerk had tucked a heart-shaped sachet into the folds of the skirt — their Valentine Sale promotion — and the dress had picked up the mingled spicy scents of crushed flowers. She held the silky softness against her for a long moment, closing her eyes. *In my sweet LIttle ALice red gown* . . . swooping, laughing, reaching for the light . . . . Lovingly, she hung the dress in the closet, where it gleamed beside the browns and greys and whites like an exotic bird in a drab winter garden. She couldn't bring herself to close the door on it. She would try it on again after a good soak in the tub, try the makeup with it.

She ran the water, sitting on the edge of the tub and

testing to make sure it was hot enough. Tomorrow at the office they'd be bursting with questions and she'd be able to give them the news first hand. It had to be some poor soul who had nobody to care if they were alive or dead; maybe the old lady she used to see sometimes in the laundry room and hadn't seen for awhile. She could hear more people congregating in the foyer, like the crowds who collected on the bridge and riverbank when there'd been a drowning. She wouldn't do that, but maybe she'd just watch from the front window so she could tell Darlene. There was a knock at her door, and she went down the hall to answer it.

The caretaker stood there, his eyes glancing shiftily past her into the apartment, as if he thought the body might be hidden there.

"Trouble's all fixed up, just letting everybody know. It was an uncapped sewer under the stairs." At her look of stunned incomprehension, he went on. "Plugged up awhile back. Fella from the City left the cap off."

She didn't answer, just stared at him. He looked uncomfortable, his eyes darting at her and away.

"Well, just wanted to let ya know. Sorry for the inconvenience." And he moved off down the hall and rapped at another door. Slowly, she closed the door, walked stiffly down the hall to the bathroom.

Alice stared at her pale face in the mirror. *Sewer gas.* Oh, God, how ridiculous. It couldn't be. They only said it was that. White. She was so white, she couldn't stand to look at herself. She picked up the bottle of foundation, opened it, plastered the tan liquid on her face. Thick. Thick. That was better. Oh, God, what a fool

they would think her at the office with her talk of dead
bodies, a dead person. With the eyeliner she drew a
heavy, black line around each eye, watched her eyes in
the mirror grow long, almond-shaped.

It was the caretaker, of course. Sly. She never had
trusted him. He was hiding something. Eyeshadow now,
carefully, eyelids becoming heavy, mysterious half-
moons of shimmering turquoise. What would she tell
them at work? Oh, dear God, he was lying, she knew
that, but if she said so they'd think she was crazy. Under
the mascara wand, her eyelashes grew long and lush and
black. Darlene would make fun of her behind her back,
pointing to her head and making fast little circles to in-
dicate that Alice was crazy. Alice had seen her doing
that, smiling at Les, how had she forgotten? Blusher.
Cheekbones emerging — high, red, exotic. Mrs. Hayes
would pity her, try to understand her. Les would feel
embarrassed for her. She couldn't bear that. Finally her
mouth; sculptured lips of deep raspberry red. Oh, it was
too much. Too much. The lipstick fell from her bloodless
fingers into the sink, a brilliant gash on the shiny white
porcelain, the silver case glittering under the light as it
rocked to a standstill. She walked into the bedroom and
lay down on top of the bedspread. She was so tired. So
cold and tired. How could she go to work tomorrow?

She didn't have to. She could quit. Her mother would
be glad to have her home, glad of the company, she
wouldn't have to go to work again, ever, if she didn't
want to. She could just rest. She needed that. Under the
mask of cosmetics, her face felt dry, stiff. She must get
up and wash it off. Later. She pulled up a quilt from
the bottom of the bed, covered herself.

She would write tomorrow. *Dear Mother. I am coming home. It is quite impossible to stay here any longer.* The air in the room was heavy with the scent of dried flowers and spices. In the shadowy closet, the red dress darkened. She turned away, stared unseeing at the ceiling. *This is difficult to explain, Mother. You see, someone has died in my apartment building and nobody is doing anything about it.*

THE LONG WAY HOME

Well, here I am. Me, Annie Johnson, seventy-five years old yesterday and never been up in a plane before, up above the clouds on my way to Hawaii.

Not that it was any surprise, winning the trip. From the moment I saw the poster in the window of the new OK Economy Store, I knew I was going to win it for Doris and me. Knew it the way you know something for no rhyme or reason. Like the way I knew that Harold was dead before they phoned me from the hospital, and nobody was expecting him to die, least of all me, standing with my hands in a sink full of dirty dishes when it happened. But I knew, and took my hands out of the water and dried them on a dishtowel to answer the phone when it rang.

Two trips a day I made to the store, ten blocks each way, to buy a quart of milk or a tin of soup or packet of tea, and to fill out my name on the entry form and drop it in the box by the door. I've always believed you should work for what you get, and it made me feel better, even though my ankles swelled and my feet hurt so I had to soak them every night, with Mrs. White fluttering around, worrying that I'd spill water on her carpet.

Those fields down there . . . all squares and rectangles of brown and buff and black as flat as a parquet floor. How strange it is to see familiar things from a totally different point of view. And those little clouds drifting across the floor like dust balls. I feel as if I could take a big mop and gather them all up in a pile, and then I could see everything there was to see for miles and miles. This is the way it must feel to be God, though God wouldn't have to do the mopping up. And His legs wouldn't hurt like mine, either.

Mrs. White laughed at me sitting every night with my fat feet soaking. "You might as well walk to Hawaii, Mrs. Johnson," she'd say; or "You wouldn't catch me walking forty blocks a day to stick my name in a box." It's true, you wouldn't. You wouldn't catch Mrs. White walking forty yards, though her legs are better than mine and she's younger, too, only seventy-one.

I went to the store that often to get away from Mrs. White as much as anything. In a little place like hers you're always under each other's feet. And it was good to get out in the air — I can always smell our stuffy old-lady smell when I open the door, and Mrs. White looks at me reproachfully when I come back, bringing the cold

air with me. Mrs. White has eyes like a Chihuahua, big
and round and moist. And accusing. In fact, she reminds
me a lot of a Chihuahua, small and bossy, though her
curly white hair is more like a poodle's. I never could
stand those dogs. Give me a mutt any day. Like old
Bugs. That poor dog missed Harold so much it was pain-
ful, carrying that old shoe around and sleeping with it,
till I couldn't stand it any more and took it away from
him. Mrs. White says old Bugs was ugly, and I guess
he was.

Mrs. White's first name is Lily. Lily White, it suits
her to a T, she's so fastidious. She was horrified about
the man in the park. There's a park I cut through
sometimes on the way to the store — it saves a block
and it's a change of scene. A couple of weeks ago there
was a rustling in the bushes, and a man stepped out right
in front of me, as naked as a jaybird if you ever saw a
jaybird wearing a crucifix and an Orangeman's ring.
Maybe that's what they call an identity crisis. I guess
I was supposed to scream or faint or run, but I'm not
the screaming or fainting type, and I'd just walked nine
blocks so I didn't have the energy to run. Besides, he
wasn't doing anything, just standing there covered in
goose pimples. "You're going to catch your death of
cold" I told him. "Go and put some clothes on." And
then I just continued on my way and left him standing
there. It was all the same to me if he wanted to go
gallivanting around with nothing on, but I did report
it to the police in case he frightened some children, or
worse, but I don't think he'd hurt anybody, really, he
didn't look the type. He looked disappointed, like a child

who wants to show you something and you won't take the time to look.

Mrs. White was so embarrassed by the questions the police asked that I swear she would have fainted if she could have managed it. Especially when I told them he had a pot belly and not much else. We had a good laugh about that, the policemen and I, and they said I was an excellent witness, noticing the Orangeman's ring. Well, my husband wore one for thirty years. Of course they advised me not to go through the park, but I'm not afraid of a bare naked Catholic.

I'll miss those trips to the store now. Once each day I'd stop and have a cup of tea at the lunch counter. They got to know me, the lunch counter girls and cashiers. "Who are you taking to Hawaii?" they'd ask me. "Can I go with you, Mrs. Johnson?" And I'd laugh and say I was taking my daughter. "But if she can't go, I'll take you," I'd tell whichever fresh-faced girl had asked. They look so nice, those girls, in their apple-green uniforms with red roses pinned to their lapels. They sometimes gave me two entry forms, or even three or four toward the end of the contest, and they'd always say "good luck" as I filled out my name in block letters. Then I'd pull my hat down and tie up my scarf for the walk home. "See you later!" they always called when I left, and when I looked in the windows between the big posters advertising specials on bananas or standing rib roasts, somebody would always smile and wave. It never seemed as far or as cold walking home from the store.

It's already the middle of November and there's no

snow worth mentioning, just a few dry skiffs, drifted into
the ruts and ditches. From up here you can't see any
snow, just miles and miles of parquet floor with here and
there a shiny slough like spilled water waiting to be
mopped up.

I always wash the floors at Mrs. White's, though Lord
knows there's not much of them, just a tiny kitchen and
the bathroom floor not much bigger than a postage
stamp. Not like my floors at home — my big old kitchen floor with the pattern worn off in places and the
yellow roses as clear and bright as new in others. And
the stairs that smelled so good and woody when they were
wet. I can't even imagine it all boarded up, without the
sun spilling in everywhere.

I think of how things used to be far more than I should;
turning over old bones in my head just makes it ache.
But they all agreed the stairs were too steep and the oil
heater too dangerous and the snow too much work and
on and on, and wasn't it wonderful for Mrs. White and
me to both have company? They can say what they like
about the convenience, it's not home and it never will
be. I knew it was a mistake that first day, when Mrs.
White took my old knitted tea cozy off the pot as if she
was touching a dirty bandage. I've never been able to
find it since, and the second cup of tea is always
lukewarm. That's what you get for trying to please
everybody but yourself. Cold tea. And it wasn't as if I
lived in the country, I had neighbors who dropped in.
Some of them had been doing it for fifty years.

It looks like the Arctic outside the window now. Solid
flat clouds like acres of drifted snow, and off in the

distance round clouds bulging up like igloos. I wouldn't be surprised to see a dogteam racing along, or a man in a frosted parka with his eyelashes frozen shut tapping on the plane window asking to come in. Like Sam McGee. I feel a lot like Sam McGee since I came to Mrs. White's, we should both have had sense enough to stay home. I used to know those Robert Service poems by heart, recited them to Doris when she was little and she loved it, especially the part about Sam smiling away in the furnace.

And I'd be wearing a smile as wide as Sam's when I told her about winning the trip. I rehearsed it in my head a hundred times. "Oh, by the way, Doris," I'd say. "I almost forgot to tell you we're going to Hawaii." And then I'd just sit back and enjoy her reaction. Doris had been to Hawaii, but that didn't matter, it was better, really, because she knew the ropes, as they say.

She had told me all about it, about the soft air that smelled of hibiscus flowers, the white beaches with the big waves whooshing in and out. And how sometimes, if you're lucky, you can see whales, far out in the water, playing. Imagine that. I thought of how I would take off my shoes and stockings and walk in the warm sand, and in the water, too, fresh and tingly on my legs.

Mrs. White said nobody would catch her making a fool of herself like that out in public. I talked too much to Mrs. White about the trip, but I was so full of it, you see, it just had to come out. Anyway, I'm getting so used to her thinking I'm a fool, it doesn't even bother me. I'm an even bigger fool than she took me for, because I'm taking Mrs. White to Hawaii with me. I still can't believe it.

I was standing right there when they drew my name, and like I said, I wasn't surprised. After the handshaking and picture-taking were over, and all the girls had hugged and kissed me and said how lucky Doris was, the manager drove me home in his nice big car. When I went in and told Mrs. White, she started to cry. Tears just kept sliding from her brown Chihuahua eyes down her face while she said she'd never had a trip like that and never would before she died. And all the time I'm standing there in my hat and coat, with the envelope still in my hand, knowing what she said was true, and suddenly feeling very old myself. Well, I asked her to go and that's that. It wasn't as if Doris had never been there, and will more than likely go again.

The Vancouver Airport is the biggest place I've ever seen. Mrs. White is upset because she thinks they've taken our valises and we'll never see them again, even though they explained to us before we left that we'd get them back in Honolulu. They're going to meet us there. Mrs. White thinks they might forget, but I don't think so, they seem to go out of their way to be nice to old women.

We've got four hours to wait, a long time to sit here, but she's tired and doesn't want me to leave her alone. Just as well, I suppose, I might not find her again, and to tell the truth I'm a little tired myself. Besides, the passing parade is a sight more interesting than any I've ever seen. People in all sizes and colors, and those ugly jet planes taking off in every direction like sharks swimming away into the blue.

Mrs. White is missing it all, sitting there with her eyes closed, her big eyes pushing out the pale lids as if she could see right through them. Watching for muggers, most likely, but the way she's hanging onto her purse they'd have to take Mrs. White, too. She's all played out from getting her hair permed and worrying about what clothes to bring and if the neighbor will be sure to water the plants. I told her why worry about how we look, nobody knows who we are. She can sit with her eyes shut for two weeks if she wants to; I'm going to walk on the hot sand in my bare feet, and listen to music, and smell the flowers hard enough to last all winter. Maybe I'll even see the whales.

And in the spring I'm going home, home to my own house, no matter what anybody says. I'll get another dog to keep me company, and when I'm ready for floors so small you can lick them clean, I'll know it, but it isn't yet. Maybe never. Maybe I'll just keel over one day in my own house, with the sun streaming in the windows and my own clutter around me. And if it happens a bit sooner there, so be it. At least I won't be mooning around like Sam McGee about what I left behind. Or jumping naked out of the bushes at unsuspecting people in the park.

It's raining here. There are lights on the landing field now, and through the wet glass those big planes wink red and blue like neon fish in a tank. And you can smell green things growing. Even from inside, you can smell the green.

SPRING

She stops on the long, grassy slope, with the wind whipping her old grey raincoat around her legs. She has stepped into a bright, happy painting. The gentle green slope is speckled with purple and yellow crocuses, with people in bright clothes and faces, and beyond it, the sage-green ocean — scattered with Seurat sailboats — dances, splinters in the sun.

The curving promenade path high above the sea is a steady passing parade: old people, there are so many here, looking grateful and faintly surprised to be feeling the warm sun on their faces; young couples with children pulling at their hands, sleeping on their backs, oblivious in carriages; sun-mellow people airing dogs, summer jackets, themselves. On the boulevard at the

top of the slope, plum trees are spraying pink froth into
the soft air, and daffodils beam their impossible yellow
in every yard. Here, on this extravagant island, it is
spring.

But it is the other element in the painting that caught
her, holds her, that pulled her from the street into this
windy scene. The sky is alive with kites. Bright, darting kites that wriggle and swim like sperm joyously trying
to impregnate its vast blue: small kites that look like kites,
and other, incredible objects that look like nothing she
has seen before: wondrous birds, exotic fishes, shooting
stars with small, bright parachutes endlessly spinning
behind. An enormous silken ladder, each rung a rainbow
hue from violet to red, sweeps low overhead, down the
rocky slope from the promenade to the beach, and out
over the splintered, dancing water. High above the boats,
a single kite launches fourteen glowing dragons with long,
whipping tails: a glorious phalanx of dragons prancing
across the windy sky.

Naomi is her name, the woman in the grey coat. She
folds her arms across her chest — the wind is cold here,
but she is only peripherally aware of it as she gazes up
at the streaming kites. She has come from the prairies,
where the wind at this time of year can freeze the skin
in seconds, and back there in the city where she has lived
most of her life, the snow is piled up under the windows
of her house, will be there still when she returns in time
for a second spring. It is the first time in her life she will
know a second spring.

She is slightly overweight, dark-haired with streaks

of grey, dark eyes fanned with lines. She is fifty years old and she looks it. Only a most discerning observer might notice, in the way she stands with the wind curved in her back, a kind of disorderly straining upward, as if she might, any moment, sever the invisible cord that holds her earthbound and soar up into the crackling blue with the fishes and dragons and bright, flashing sperm.

The woman, Naomi, has a lover. For half of her life she had a husband. Now she has a lover.

The man she was married to for twenty-five years loved order above all things. He loved her in his way, and she loved him in his way also. So it started and so it kept on.

She has been alone in her life, her bed, since his orderly departure from them two years before. At exactly ten a.m. on a Friday morning he put his head down on his desk and tidily died, just after his secretary brought around a cup of the herbal tea he drank each morning to keep his bowels regular. He didn't spill the tea, or the photographs of his wife and son, who looked from their silver frames as he stopped seeing.

She missed his presence terribly, of course — across the dinner table, in his seat at the symphony — but she did not really miss the neat, infrequent couplings that had scarcely disturbed the sheets. Once, long ago, she had wanted more, had tried to tell him, to place his hand thus and so, came to him once after wine with her nipples rouged, but his shocked, retreating eyes had sent her away, face flaming, to rub out the rouge, and more.

She told herself that part of her life was over, that

it didn't matter, and believed it. Until she came here,
where everything was so lush and moist and bursting
as to be almost indecent. Until she was fifty.

She walks every day here, walks and walks and always
she ends at the sea. Like all prairie people, she loves the
ocean for its flatness, its distances, but also for its
differences.

She saw him there sometimes, sawing driftwood and
loading it in an old truck, his brown beard streaked with
grey and runnelled by the wind. He wore a navy jacket
and toque, and his eyes were full of distance, like a
sailor's. They spoke of many things, as strangers will
sometimes, and she looked at his hands, chapped and
good on the wood. Often, on cold days, they were the
only people on the beach.

She began to dream about his hands, the rough skin
catching on hers. She dreamed of parting his beard and
touching the pulse in his pale throat.

He told her how to recognize the different woods —
birch, willow, pine — he makes things with it, sells it
for firewood. He told her about this place, that was not
always his place, gave her coffee from his thermos. One
day he told her this: you have a very sensuous mouth,
and went on sawing. When he straightened up there was
sawdust in his beard and the hairs in his nostrils. He
reached for the thermos and she took his cold hand and
pressed it to her face, opening its palm to her warm,
moist breath. And between her breasts and throat was
a gushing like warm, fluid quicksilver.

Driving down the wet, tree-heavy road to his house,

in the truck cab that smelled of damp wool and wound-
ed wood, the quicksilver spread. He put his hand on her
leg and she slid it around to the inside of her thigh, warm-
ing it between her legs. She felt no surprise at her actions,
only faint amusement that there was none.

He cuts wood on the beach every Monday.

There is no one to tell. She longs to tell it, for it seems
like the most important thing that has ever happened
to her. She has friends here and, between Mondays, she
goes out to dinner, to the library, museums and, one
memorable night, to *Tosca.* Cavaradossi's shoulders, his
hands as he holds Tosca's face, remind her of him, and
there in the stuffy, velvet theatre, her throat is thick with
wanting. My lover holds my face like that, she wants
to tell her companion, wants to lean over and tell the
old lady fanning herself in the seat ahead. She thinks
of the king's barber whispering his secret to the reeds,
Chekhov's cabby telling his sorrow to his horse. I have
a lover, she whispers inside her head as she walks, talks,
breathes. His beard smells of pine. His belly is flat and
beautiful. He makes my juices run.

She sees with amazement that an entire element of
her life has been neglected, left out, like a painting with
blank white canvas where the sky should be. She longs
to talk of that to someone. She almost does, over tea one
day with a woman she had known a long time, but something about the determined tailoring of the woman's suit
and mouth stops her.

One lazy afternoon, as she browses in a second-hand

bookstore, with a lowering sky outside and rain drizzling the windows, this happens: Like a furnace door has opened somewhere inside her, a sudden warmth gathers, intensifies, rises, until she is engulfed in heat that pushes from inside and outside her body at once. A fierce, dry, kiln-like heat that must surely bubble the blood in her veins, and even then it doesn't stop. She looks with surprise at the frizzy girl talking on the phone behind the desk; at the tortoise-shell cat in the window stretching, retracting, dozing again; at two blue-haired, umbrella-shaded women passing by in the street; and finally, gradually, the heat subsides. She feels it trapped inside her belted raincoat. Her skin feels tender, as if she'd got too close to a fire.

So, she thinks. So.

Her sublet apartment is on the second floor of an old three-storey building, its large, corner windows slatted with venetian blinds. One of the windows looks down on a main thoroughfare to the high school a block away. Punk fashion is in and Naomi finds herself watching for a short, sassy girl whose inventiveness knows no bounds. Tee shirts, knee socks, shoes, hair, all change color with equal ease, and even on drenching days, with her tattered Dickens tailcoat and crested head, she flutters on bright legs like a tropical bird.

The other window looks out on the Oak Bay Lodge, an old folks' home. Senior citizens' home, someone would be sure to correct her, but the inmates next door do not look like senior citizens, they look like old people.

The old woman directly across feeds the crows that

complain endlessly in the black oaks that line the street. It must be against the rules, she does it surreptitiously, flattening her reedy body against the wall that divides the balconies, darting out to lay chunks of bread on the railing. They swoop in, scrabbling, flapping, filling the air in front of her with their blue-black wings, their greedy beaks.

Volunteers take the old people walking. The walkers never seem to talk to the pale omens who clutch their hands or clothes, but they slow their steps to accommodate those scurrying beside or behind. One extremely large woman always takes three people at once — a fragile, very straight man who holds her elbow in a courtly way, as if he is helping her across the street, and two old women holding the tail of her raincoat out behind her. The large woman's steps are slow and stately. They go by often, like a strange wedding procession that never achieves the altar.

The crow woman never walks, she sits behind the glass of her balcony door, looking out, sits there alone. Naomi looks at the woman behind the glass. Soon, she thinks. Soon I will make love in a room with a fire.

There is more. The smell of clams and vegetables and spices simmering in a pot; sea wind pushing hard at her, smelling of ozone and weeds and things in shells; the dark shine of laurel in the rain.

And more. Yellow spirea by a glistening black rock; sun caught in the pink and mauve iridescence of a pigeon's throat, in the fanning white tailfeathers of gulls hovering overhead, their cries filling the air. Everywhere, the keening cries of gulls. And once, in a downtown square in the rain, an ancient plum tree in full bloom, delicate pink blossoms bursting even from its dark trunk, exploding all up and down the rough wet bark.

As she walks at the edge of the water, her pockets bulge with smooth stones and bits of colored glass, washed opaque and strangely beautiful by sand and sea. He gives her a seashell with a pearly interior, as smooth to her tongue as the inside of his bottom lip. Her storage closet rattles with walking sticks she picks up, liking the feel of them in her hand. Perhaps she will take them home to burn, smell the ocean in her fireplace.

Once, because she still wants to tell it, she scratches in the wet sand at the water's edge, I LOVE. She stands for a moment, stick poised, then walks on. It is enough.

And everywhere the flowers, pushing up from the black earth, burning in the trees, juxtaposed in a profusion of color and sweet spicy smells outside the corner stores. She keeps a jug of flowers, always fresh, in the room with the windows that look both ways.

Now, as she stands on this windy hillside, she counts the Mondays that are left and finds them few. Finds also that it doesn't matter. The landscape she will return to is still bleak, but in protected places there — under the windows of her house, under snow and frozen earth — hyacinth bulbs are dreaming purple dreams, and tulips will soon swell redly from last year's skins.

Even without that promise, for the woman with the warmth of spring on her face, it is enough. For here, high above the spangled ocean, gulls and rainbows and

streaming dragons ride the wind. And up there, just
catching the breeze, a rose; its silken petals shading from
the faintest blush of pink, to deep, glowing red. A
glorious soaring rose, that opens and opens to the sun
its crimson centre, pulsing against the ringing blue of
the sky.

MICK & I & HONG KONG HEAVEN

Mick has been dry for two months, not so much as a sip, and if I believed in miracles the way these A.A. people claim they do, I'd have to say this was one. I can't say I care for it.

It all started with a twelve-step call, and if you don't know what that is I'll tell you, in case anybody ever wants to make one on you. A twelve-step call is where a couple of alcoholics in A.A. go and see someone and try to get him to stop drinking. Well, they only go if they're asked, and I phoned them so I feel responsible, but I never meant them to take over his life like this — I never thought he'd stop completely, like some temperance nut. I only wanted him to slow down and stop wanting to kill himself.

Mick is a lovely person most of the time, which is why I have lived with him for a year and a half, I figure most of the time is as good as anybody's going to get. But now everything's changed, and I just want things the way they used to be. I can't stand the way he looks at me now when I have a drink, like a missionary who's caught a cannibal boiling somebody's head in a pot. A missionary who's going to teach you to eat berries instead. But even though Mick on the wagon is not one of my favorite sights, I have to admit he seems happy, I suppose because he's found all those other people in the same boat, or on the same wagon, I guess you'd say. Anyways, the day I met him, A.A. was the farthest thing from his mind.

I was laying in the back yard on my day off, sunning myself in my purple bikini and sipping a cold beer, which is the only way to spend a hot July day if you don't have a pool or a summer cottage. I was reading this Harlequin romance about a girl who is hired by a real bastard to pretend she is his fiancee in Hong Kong, a job she takes to keep her brother out of jail because he stole money from this guy whose fiancee she's pretending to be. Of course the real bastard is tall, dark and handsome and hard as a stick. All of the men in those books are hard — hard lips, hard stomachs, hard jaws, not an ounce of fat on any of them, even though they're always swilling down champagne and eating all kinds of fattening stuff in fancy restaurants where the headwaiter knows them. Another thing they always are is rich.

Anyways, this guy treats her like dirt because she's just a mousy parson's daughter, until she gets into all

the fancy clothes he bought her so she'd look like a rich
man's fiancee and then she's a knockout. Of course she
hates him and has the hots for him at the same time.

Well, like I said, I'm just laying there minding my
own business when Henry starts barking like crazy. I
shared the house with two other nurse's aides, and when
we rented it, this evil little chihuahua called Henry came
with the deal. I don't blame them for leaving Henry —
he was fat and had no hair and he just sat around on
his bare behind growling to himself with a crazy look
in his little bug eyes.

So Henry is going bananas having something to actually bark at, and I'm yelling at him to stick it in his ear,
when this long, hard man in a green meter-reading
uniform ambles around the corner of the house. He looks
me over real good and his eyes light up like maybe Sask
Power wires them for electricity.

"Hi, mate," he says to Henry, who is trying to tear
his pantleg off.

"GrrrrrOWOWOWOWOW! GrrrrOWOWOW-
OW!" Henry replies, around a mouthful of green
material. His little bow legs are braced on the sidewalk
and his nose is wrinkled all the way up to his forehead.

"Aow, come on mate, you'll give yourself an ulcer,"
says this movie actor pretending to be a meter reader,
and he pats old Henry on the head.

"Growl, growl," says Henry, but you can tell his
heart's not in it any more, and before you know it this
guy is down on his haunches scratching Henry on the
bare belly, which he is wriggling at the sky.

Then this beautiful man is looking over at me like
maybe I might need my belly scratched. "Helloaw there,

luv,'' he says, And then he smiles.

It was the smile that did it. That and the bluest eyes this side of Paul Newman. Anyways, before you can say kilowatt hour, he's sitting beside me on the blanket, pouring a bottle of my beer down his throat.

"Ahhh. That hits the old proverbial dry spot," he says. I *think* that's what he said, he talks like the Beatles only moreso, and half of it goes right past me. He stretches out his long legs and leans back on his elbows like he's planning to stay awhile.

"Where did you get this magnificent beast?" he asks, scratching Henry on the bald head. Henry thinks he's died and gone to heaven. So I tell Mick about my roommates and my job and pretty soon we're talking up a storm and I go get us another beer.

Now you hear a lot about women's throats being beautiful, but I have never seen a lovelier sight than the muscles sliding under the smooth, tanned throat of this meter reader as he tips back his head and guzzles my beer. I got so fascinated watching it that I just kept offering him one after another and I never in my life saw anybody drink like he could. Not even my old man. It was like he was trying to put out a fire in his stomach.

"Whoever said redheads can't wear purple are loony," he says. He was spending considerable time looking down the top of my bikini, in a nice way.

I was looking him over, too; in fact I couldn't stop looking. He was a real classy guy, even if the green uniform was a little baggy on him.

"What's the book about?" he asks, picking up *Hong Kong Heaven* off the blanket. So I told him about the

churchmouse and the bastard who would turn out not
to be one, and about the churchmouse's crooked brother
and their old sick father, the parson, who she's trying
to protect, and this guy is killing himself laughing. Pretty
soon we're laughing together about everything under the
sun. He was from London, England, and I just loved
the way he talked. He nicknamed me Bikky right there,
because of the bikini, and he's called me that ever since.
My name is Angela.

He took off his jacket right away, it being hotter than
Hades in the sun, and after awhile he takes off his shirt,
too. He has a lovely chest with WHY ME written on
it. I couldn't believe it. Not really written on it, *scarred*
on it in thin white capital letters, as plain as anything
against his tan: WHY ME

Looking at a guy with a question on his chest should
have freaked me out, I suppose, but it didn't. I didn't
even mention it, not wanting to scare him away, and
he didn't either. I sort of liked that, too — it takes a
lot of cool to sit around with a big question carved on
your front and not feel like you have to explain it. I
always explain everything. Even when people aren't the
least bit interested. Anyhow, I didn't give a rip what
it meant as long as it didn't mean he was gay.

"Bikky," he says, "you are such a lovely surprise.
You remind me of a girl I went to law school with."

I felt suddenly shy. Law school. I thought he was just
an ordinary guy. He acted like an ordinary person,
though, and pretty soon I was feeling comfortable again.

"How come you're reading meters when you've been
to law school?" I asked.

"Oh, I don't know," he says. "I think I passed the wrong bar exams." And he laughs. God, he was beautiful when he laughed.

Well, he kept on drinking and talking and looking down my bikini top like he had nothing else to do and I started feeling nice and warm, which had nothing whatever to do with the sun which had sank over the other side of the house by the time we finished the third beer. Besides, if I'd been sunning the parts that felt warm I'dve been arrested.

When the case was empty, we jumped in the City Power truck and went to get some more, and before the girls got home from the evening shift, he had talked me right out of my bikini and read my meter, if you get my meaning. He said it was the highest one he ever read, and he must've read lots of them. And ever since, it's been ticking just for him.

The next day I moved in with Mick, who lived in a big old house on the other side of town, with a scruffy little yard and a whole lot of funny people living on the second and third floors. It was Mick's house and he rented out rooms. I gradually got used to them all, even the scaly little man with the skin condition worse than Henry's.

At first, life with Mick was fantastic, just one big lovely party, and I'd do it again in a minute. I was crazy about him then and I still am, and nobody likes a party better than me.

Mick got fired for drinking beer in my back yard while he was supposed to be reading those other meters, and for forgetting to take the truck back. He forgot everything once he started to drink, which was something I was to find out. After awhile he got a job as a waiter in a classy restaurant, but one night he got into the cooking sherry and told a fat lady she couldn't have any dessert, so they fired him, too.

"Well, you should have seen her, Bikky. She must have weighed three hundred pounds," he told me, sitting at our kitchen table in the black waiter's suit and white shirt he looked so terrific in. The kitchen table was where we talked over everything. "I just told her to be a good girl and forget about dessert."

"Oh, no." I could see it all, and nearly died laughing. "Was she mad?"

"Mad? She was ready to kill me. So was her skinny little husband, and I was trying to do him a favor." Mick looked injured.

"Do you suppose he likes her that way? There was a story about a couple like that in the National Enquirer. He even bought her all this junk to eat every time she tried to go on a diet. He was afraid if she got thin she'd . . ." But Mick wasn't interested in discussing motivation, and he hated the National Enquirer.

"Oh, well," he said, getting up to pour a drink. "She'll roll on him some night and that will be the end of the silly little sod. Serve him right, too."

It didn't matter much if Mick worked or not because his folks were rich and sent him money all the time. He laughed and called himself a remittance man, but I got the feeling he didn't really think it was funny. They'd told him not to come home till he quit drinking, though his mother wrote him every week in her aristocratic handwriting with real ink, not ballpoint. I wondered what she wrote about, but Mick didn't say and I would never read his mail. Their loss was my gain was the way I looked at it. I didn't want him to ever go back.

His folks said he was alcoholic and I thought that was really retarded, I mean I liked to drink almost as much as Mick. Well, it was like I loved to drink but Mick really *needed* to drink sometimes. In the middle of the night, even, if he'd been talking to Ralph on the big white telephone. That was Mick's expression for puking up your guts in the toilet, and the first time I heard him being sick, it did sound like he was calling RAAAAALPH! RAAAAALPH! Mick says you only have to worry if Ralph starts talking back. But I didn't think much about Mick's drinking one way or the other till I heard the tea party story.

We were sitting around the kitchen table having a beer, Mick and I and Buddy, the scaly little man from upstairs. Well, you never had ''a'' beer with Mick, but you know what I mean.

''Did I ever tell you about the time I livened up my mum's tea party?'' Mick asked.

Buddy loved Mick's stories, and was grinning away in anticipation, shedding silvery scales of skin onto his old grey sweater. They gleamed here and there when he moved, like he might be turning into a fish.

''I used to play bridge,'' he said.

Poor old Buddy was as dumb as a bag of hammers, so that was hard to imagine. Mick said he'd fried his brain with rubbing alcohol and shoe polish. His teeth were a kind of mahogany brown, so that must've been his favorite flavor. Buddy has one thing he says to everything: "Yessir, that's quite a thing," he'll say. It's surprising how often it's appropriate.

"Well," Mick went on, "Mum used to have her church ladies in for tea every Tuesday fortnight. And sometimes, if I was in my cups, she'd lock me in my room upstairs. Poor old duck was afraid I'd embarrass her."

"I couldn't stand to be locked in," I said. Sometimes Mick's stories bothered me, even if they were funny.

"Yessir, that's quite a thing." Buddy shook his crusty little head, which looked something like a baby bird's.

"And if I got crashing around up there, she'd just tell her friends that Mick was fixing something upstairs, and then she'd go ahead and bid a grand slam." That's what made Mick's stories so good — he always imagined the parts he couldn't see, like he couldn't know about the grand slam, really, but it helped the story.

"This one day she locked me in, I was needing a drink like I'd just crawled across the desert." As if that reminded him, he held up his emptty bottle and grinned at me. I got up and got three bottles out of the fridge.

"I paced around up there," Mick says, "vibrating like a hummingbird, and when I couldn't stand it any longer, I jumped out."

I stopped in my tracks halfway back to the table. "Jumped out where?" I asked.

"Out the flaming window," Mick says, laughing. "Out the second-storey window right past the tea party in the drawing room."

"Jesus." I said.

Heavy drinking was nothing new to me. The only reason my father wasn't the town drunk was because we lived in the country, but he wouldn't jump out a two-storey window to get a drink. He might fall out of one if he had enough, but that was different.

Mick was laughing, and Buddy was cackling away, showing all his shiny brown teeth. "Yessir, that's quite a . . ."

"Were you hurt?" I interrupted. Sometimes Buddy got on my nerves.

"Hell no, luv. God looks after fools and drunks. I just took off like a shot for the pub, with all of them staring at me over their teacups like they'd just seen an alien landing."

"Yessir, them aliens is quite the things."

"That's when my folks sent for the boys in white," Mick said. He always laughed about being in the loony bin, saying how good he was at making belts and icing cookies. It mustn't have been very funny, though, because that's where he carved up his chest with the razor blade. It was when he ran away from there that they sent him to Canada. To me. Like a Harlequin romance, in a way, him coming from another country and being so handsome and all, and just walking into my life out of the blue.

Except you never found people like Buddy in Harlequin romances. Or anywhere else, that I know of. Mick had found him down on the river bank, with one skinny arm wrapped around a tree so he wouldn't slide into the river, drinking out of a paper bag. Well, out of a *bottle* that was in a paper bag, not actually out of a . . . see, that's what I mean about over-explaining. Or Frankie, the girl who lived upstairs, who carved up her face with a broken thermometer on one of her drug trips. Frankie was beautiful, even with the scars. But they weren't all burnouts. There was a short, dark guy on the third floor who wore bright red pants and glasses with rhinestones on them. I asked Mick what he did and he said he got shot out of a cannon, but he actually worked at Safeway's, I saw him there after.

There was usually a party going on somewhere in that house, two or three times a week, but Mick was drinking more and more just with me. Or alone.

One night he went to meet an old friend at the bar, and I stayed home and went to bed. He got in about four a.m. and when I turned on the bedside light he was standing at the foot of the bed, looking like he'd seen a ghost.

"Bikky. Thank God it's you."

"Well, who else would it be?" I said, reaching for my cigarettes as Mick sat down on the edge of the bed. I could feel the cold air coming off him and he looked half frozen.

"Where's your jacket?" I asked, but he just shrugged. He was always losing things. His jeans were muddy and his good navy sweater was covered with bits of dirt and fuzz. He was shaking like a leaf, and I lit a cigarette and gave it to him.

"Oh, God, Bikky, I've had a horrid experience. I was sitting in Fast Freddie's with Michael, just talking over old times, and I must have blacked out, because all at once I'm washing my hands in a strange bathroom, and

I don't have a clue where I am. Or how I got there.''
Everybody has a drinking blackout now and then, like
not remembering where they parked the car, that sort
of thing, but Mick had bad ones.

"It was a half bath off a bedroom and a man and
woman were sleeping in the bed. I'd never seen them
before." Mick put his head down on his knees and was
quiet for a long time, with his hands crossed on top of
his dark hair and the cigarette burning right down to
his fingers. I took it and butted it.

"What did you do?" I imagined screams; a fight;
police.

"I crawled out of there on my belly, that's what I did.
It took me an age to get out, I was so terrified of waking
them. And the rug was filthy."

"Well, I guess she wasn't expecting company," I said,
starting to pick the red fuzz and junk off his sweater and
putting it in the ashtray.

"That's not the worst part," Mick said, his voice
sounding kind of strange and empty. "When I first saw
my face in that bathroom mirror, I didn't know who I
was."

He looked like he still didn't know. I held the covers
open. "Come in and get warm," I said. I didn't know
what else to do.

After that Mick got worse. He was drinking more and
enjoying it less, as they say in the cigarette ads, and he
was starting to look like death warmed over. He didn't
care if he ever ate when he was on a bat, and he was
talking to Ralph a lot on the big white telephone.

He sat and stared into space a lot, too, like he was

looking into a big black tunnel he was going to have to walk through by himself, and I was afraid to go to work sometimes and leave him. He tried to kill himself once, sawing away at his wrists with an old, dull disposable razor that was plugged full of leg and armpit hair. He was shaking too hard to do it right, anyway. God, it was awful how he'd shake. Sometimes I would wake up with the vibrations of the bed, and he'd be sitting on the edge with the sweat running into his eyes, trying to hold a glass of scotch steady. If he could get it down and it stayed there, he'd eventually fall asleep.

Mick's last drunk was not that spectacular, really. He just kept it up for days, till he kind of drank himself sober, and one night he asked me to take him for a drive in the country. It was one of those wild, windy nights in early spring, and I didn't have to go to work until eleven.

Mick looked ghastly, so thin and white, and we stopped at the A&W on the way out of town, where he drank a large vanilla shake to settle his stomach. He was talking a lot, not drunk talk, but excitable, like some-body'd wound him up with a key.

"God, I feel good tonight, Bikky. I feel so good. My head is clear as a bell." He tapped himself on the side of the head — "ding dong, Avon calling" — and he laughed and laughed. "Oh, Bikky my darlin', the times they are a-changing. I can feel it in the air."

"What times? What's changing?"

I had driven out the Regina highway and it was good, being in the country again. The snow was melting fast in the fields, and in the ditches the first patches of green were showing through. Mick was babbling on about how

141

things were going to change, about people being in control of their own destinies, didn't I agree, about how he'd
screwed up, he'd admit that, but it wasn't too late to
change things — he'd go back to school, paint the house
inside and out, go to New York to see an old schoolmate
who had a law firm. I'd never seen him so excited,
though he wasn't making much sense. Every once in a
while he got on this kick about changing everything.

"Spring is here," I said, trying to change the subject.

Mick rolled down his window and breathed in the
spring air like somebody who's been shut away for a long
time.

"So it is," he says, sounding surprised. "It really is
spring." And he didn't say anything for quite awhile,
just looked out the window at the prairie, tinged all rosy
from the setting sun. With the warm wind pushing
behind us, it felt as if the car might leave the road any
moment and soar off over the fields. I reached into my
purse for the mickey I'd brought because I knew Mick
would need a drink, and had a good swig before passing it over.

"A toast to spring," I said.

"Bikky, do you ever feel that you're wasting your
life?" Just like that, out of the blue he asks me if I'm
wasting my life.

"No," I said, louder than I meant to. "There's no
reason why I should."

"I don't know," says Mick, the way people say it
when they really do know something. He hadn't had a
drink, which was strange, and he was holding the mickey
on his knees, like he didn't want to get too close to it.

"I've been doing a lot of thinking lately."

I reached for the mickey. Sometimes I liked it better when Mick didn't think. I didn't answer, hoping it wasn't one of his morbid spells coming on.

"I think we should quit drinking, Bikky."

"We?" I said. "*We*? Speak for yourself, mate." I'd picked up some of Mick's expressions. I always do that when I like somebody a lot. "You just need to cut down, that's all. You don't have to get carried away."

The road to Last Mountain Lake was just ahead and I hung a left there, thinking to stop somewhere along it and get a beer out of the trunk. I shouldn't be drinking so much when I had to go to work, but Mick was making me nervous.

"Just cut down," I said again. "That's all you have to do." I glanced at him. He looked worse than before — whiter, with an expression I couldn't read.

"Ah, maybe you're right, luv," Mick finally said, reaching for the bottle, but he sounded depressed again.

It was getting dark, but you could still see. "Look at the ducks," I said, pointing to a shiny slough in the stubble field beside the road. I wanted to get him cheered up before I had to leave him and go to work. "The ducks are back." There were quite a few of them swimming around, one with its head in the water and just its bum sticking out.

Mick didn't answer, and when I looked over at him, he was crying. He was staring out the window, with the bottle on his lap, and the tears were just running down his face. He didn't even bother to wipe them away, and he looked so . . . so *defeated*, somehow.

The road was terrible, up and down and full of pot-
holes, and I was watching for a side road to turn around.
We had just come to the bottom of a long, long hill when
Mick yells at me to stop, and he was out behind the car
before it stopped rolling.

I looked back and I'll never forget it.

Mick was just standing there in that howling wind,
not bent over or anything, with a great white flag of
vomit blowing out of his mouth and off to the side. It
went on and on and on, and I couldn't look away, it
was so strange. Mick's pale face, and that big white ban-
ner of puke blowing in the dark.

It was finally over and he got back in the car, leaning
his head against the window.

"That's it, Bikky," he said. After awhile he said it
again. "That's it."

We drove all the way home with the windows open,
he smelled so bad, and I knew he was horribly ashamed.

Back home he sat at the kitchen table for the longest
time, with a face as white as death. He looked like a man
with his whole life passing in front of his eyes. Then he
asked me to call A.A.

I took off his shirt and washed him up right there at
the table, from a basin. I felt so sad, like a foster mother
who's waiting for the adoption agency to come and take
a child she loves more than anything. It was stupid,
really, I don't know why I felt like that, but I did. They
rang the doorbell just before I left for work, and it was
hard to be civil to them. At the same time I knew he
couldn't go on like that. He would kill himself.

Well, like I said, Mick has been two whole months

without a drink. I figured once he got out of that treatment centre they hauled him off to, he'd be able to have a few now and then, just enough to have a good time. But he's off to those meetings nearly every night, or those A.A. guys are sitting around the kitchen table, swilling down coffee and laughing like a bunch of idiots. I never heard people laugh like they do. I sneak a beer up to Buddy's room sometimes when they're there, but he's not your ideal drinking companion, and I've even seen them eyeing poor old Buddy like they might be thinking of recruiting him. Well, I guess he could sit around saying Yessir, that's quite a thing, at A.A. meetings as well as anywhere else.

Frankie's in the hospital, she o.d.'d again, and I heard Mick talking to them about going up to see her. He wants to sober up the whole world. Starting with me.

I can't get over the change in Mick. I've even seen him down on his knees, in the bathroom, praying. I bet it surprised the hell out of Ralph.

And he's looking fantastic, even better than the day he ambled around the corner of the house into my life. He's talking about going back to university this fall and getting a master's degree in law. He's talked to his folks a couple of times and I think they're starting to want him back. He says he loves me, but I don't know. I guess things are just happening too fast.

The other night Mick and I went to a second-hand bookstore, where Mick spent about a hundred dollars. That's the way we spend our evenings now, going to second-hand bookstores. Or having coffee with people. I wonder that those A.A.'s ever get a wink of sleep, or that they haven't all died of caffeine poisoning long ago. If you ask me, they'd be better off to have a drink now and then. Anyways, at the bookstore I saw that Harlequin romance I was reading the day I met Mick, and I just stood there and sort of scanned it through to the end.

Tall, Dark and Handsome and the churchmouse sail off in a sampan at the end, kissing behind the sail, with this Chinese guy filling up their glasses every time they turn around. Nobody ends up puking in the wind.

THE NIGHT WATCHMAN

I am like a pelican of the wilderness:
I am like an owl of the desert.

For I have eaten ashes like bread,
and mingled my drink with weeping

Psalm 102:6, 9

They came on a hot summer morning just as the Children's Parade slowly wound its way along College Drive and down the Twenty-fifth Street Bridge. In the clear, windy sky, high above the snapping flags, the noise and glitter of the parade, they came — wave after wave of enormous white birds, like a squadron of bombers sweeping toward the bridge.

"Cranes!" someone shouted. "Whooping cranes!"

Matthew looked up, and something caught at his heart.

"Geese!" someone else called. "No, cranes!" another. But they couldn't be cranes. There were too many of them.

The parade became confused, disorderly, a forest of arms pointing up as more and more of the huge birds soared over the bridge, the sun caught in their snowy white bodies, their immense, black-bordered wings.

Shriners, resplendent in red, green and gold, were poised at the top of the bridge. From tiny motorcycles, shiny red convertibles, wooden hobby horses, they looked up. Behind them on the parade route that wound up past the university campus, a gigantic Orphan Annie stared round-eyed across the river, her arm around her faithful dog Sandy. Beyond the Annie float, the Bonnie Bluebells in sweltering plaid gamely marched in place, flushed cheeks bulging. Droning bars of "Amazing Grace" carried faintly to the bridge.

On the bridge, the Sesame Street float was stalled. Big Bird had stopped dead, his yellow feathers plastered to his skinny frame, and his bill pointing skyward. Count Dracula stopped counting and stared up, his black cape billowing around his small, white face, as the last of the birds passed over the bridge. Above Rotary Park, their reconnaissance flight complete, they banked into the wind, spiralling higher and higher till the sky was filled with brilliant white flight, then streamed back towards the bridge in a long, straight line.

"Pelicans," said a voice, filled with wonder. "They're

pelicans." And Matthew Winter realized that the voice was his.

The parade was forgotten as everyone stared up. "Seventeen, eighteen, nineteen, twenty," shouted the Count, who had recovered enough to seize the opportunity. The birds flew lower on their way back, each pair of outspread wings spanning at least seven feet. "Twenty-five, twenty-six, twenty-seven . . ." Matthew heard the wind in their feathers, and noted with amusement the relaxed S-shape of head and neck in flight, which gave the huge birds a droll, "just along for the ride" look. As the last one flew over, Matthew was working his way through the crowd to the side of the bridge for an unobstructed view of their departure.

Downriver, past where the glistening water slid over the dam, was a narrow green island dotted with gulls. As the strains of "Amazing Grace" grew louder, the pelicans skimmed toward the island, losing altitude like planes approaching an aircraft carrier, and one by one they braked and landed, turning the island into a magical summer snowdrift.

As the last float rolled past the end of the bridge, Matthew veered to the right, escaping the crowd, and headed along the river bank toward the snowdrift. Chunks of it were breaking off and floating out into the water, and when Matthew reached the place where the river spilled, smooth and shining, over the dam, the big birds were forming a long line there to feed. Stationing themselves a few feet apart and about the same distance back from the dam, they patiently waited for the churning water to serve up fish.

One pelican fished far from the rest and near the cement apron where Matthew stood. Close enough for him to see the water sluicing from its long orange bill, see fish disappear inside the veiny, flesh-colored pouch. Close enough to observe what a queer, unlovely creature it was when not in flight. It was odd, their coming this late in the summer. Something must have gone wrong at the nesting ground.

Gulls wheeled excitedly over the pelicans, "klee-aah klee-aah klee-ah's mingling with the crashing of water over the dam. Matthew smiled as he sat down to watch.

Matthew Winter was a solitary man. He worked alone, walked alone, slept alone, and sometimes, when something seen or remembered made the need to be touched too insistent, he would quiet it himself, feeling, afterward, more desolate than ever.

Matthew once had a wife, but she had left years ago. Because of his drinking, she said. Because he was ugly and unlovable, he heard. Clothing hung on his tall frame like a suit on a rack, and his big ears stood almost at right angles to his head. His nose was large and squashy, the kind of nose a child might fashion from plasticene. Matthew suffered still, at fifty-six, from a stomach-knotting shyness he'd never been able to overcome.

Alcohol had eased it for years until, like a skillful thief who takes only small change at first, it gradually robbed him of everything. His deadly earnest attempt to kill himself — he'd failed even at that — had brought him in a screeching ambulance from his rooming house to the hospital. To a room where hypos grew striped hides,

malevolent eyes, flicking tongues; where a man in a blue
coverall vacuumed the shining hallway with a large
python; and where once, horrifyingly, an orderly pulled
a newborn snake from its nest in a cigarette case, placed
it between his lips, and set fire to it with a gold lighter.

"Murderer!" Matthew had screamed, as everything
slid out of control once again.

"Murderer!" as they folded him inside a straight
jacket one more time.

"Crazy old coot," said the orderly to the nurse. He
puffed on the snake, which sizzled in a ghastly way.

"Crazy as a shithouse rat," said the orderly, whisk-
ing out of the room.

And all night long, sopping wet rats in straight jackets
walked up out of the toilet and around the room, leaving damp little tracks and puddles everywhere. Matthew
laughed till he hurt at the paranoid expressions on their
little rat faces. That was the night he stopped screaming and started getting better.

From the hospital, he went to a treatment centre, and
then, at his psychiatrist's recommendation, to a halfway
house for recovering alcoholics. He'd been at Hope
Haven a month now.

Living with fourteen other people had not eased his
sense of isolation. The empty space inside him was not
made smaller by the way the light fell on the plastic fur-
niture, by footsteps sighing down the hall to the cigarette-
stained bathroom, by the slap slap slap of cards at four
in the morning. He was uneasy with the too-fast friend-
ships, the souls laid bare under the awful light, the
chipped cups.

But most of all he was distressed by the aura of failed past that weighted the air in the rooms, shadowed the corners. Even the term halfway house made him ill at ease. He didn't know where he was halfway to, or from, and couldn't bring himself to care. Soon he would move, he kept telling himself. But somehow he didn't.

The parade was the topic of conversation as they sat around the big kitchen table that evening. Supper had been especially bad because Ruby, the cook, had met her estranged husband that afternoon to talk about a divorce. At first Matthew thought Ruby was a widow, because she always dressed completely in black, and she cried as she stirred things, her black pockets bulging with lumpy, wet kleenex. The food reflected Ruby's emotional state. Soggy, tasteless casseroles, cakes that slumped tiredly in upon themselves.

"Yessir, a lot of work goes into those parades," Wilf said. "I'll never forget seeing the Rose Bowl parade in '62. Right out of this world, man."

"Was everything made of roses?" asked Ruby, from her stool by the stove, where she sat smoking a cigarette and dropping ashes in the pan under the electric burner.

"Everything but the people," Wilf said. "Well, maybe not all roses, but flowers. Every damn thing made of flowers."

"I don't believe that," said Rafe, in his flat, un-equivocal voice. Rafe was Cree, about twenty years old, with long black hair held back in a ponytail. He was a determined loner, who appeared to find Wilf's cheerful babble especially irritating.

"That's your privilege, man," Wilf said, going on to describe the wonders of the Rose Bowl.

The kitchen didn't depress Matthew like the rest of the house. The light was different there, the walls a soft yellow, probably the only room where the paint hadn't been donated by a paint store at inventory time. Some vestiges of the gracious home it had once been still remained, in the leaded glass panels in the front door and upstairs hallway, the oak doors and heavy glass doorknobs.

"I liked the Cinderella float best today," said Verla, the beautiful seventeen-year-old with the most perfect teeth Matthew had ever seen. "I loved the ugly sisters."

"Yeah, I thought one of 'em looked a lot like you, Verla." Wilf grinned at her and then around the table. With his soft, brown beard and little, moccasined feet, Wilf looked like he belonged in a fairy tale himself. Under a bridge, maybe. "How'd you like Snow White in her glass coffin?"

"Saran wrap coffin, you mean," said Ruby, leaning over the table with the last of the pudding in the pan. Under the light, her yellow hair sprang black and grey at the roots. "Who wants to clean this up?"

Harvey grinned up at her and she plopped the spongy chocolate mess onto his plate and went back to her stool. She leaned over to tip the coffee maker toward her cup, and was rewarded by a thin, dark dribble. She gave it a bleak look.

"Son of a bitch," said Ruby. "I really needed that cup of coffee."

Matthew got up and dumped the coffee grounds into

the big garbage container, rinsed out the coffee maker and started to refill it. Ruby sniffled, and Matthew remembered, too late, that kindness always made her cry.

"Weren't the pelicans wonderful?" said Ruth, a sad-looking woman about Matthew's age. It was the first time she'd joined in a conversation since her arrival, a week ago.

"Well, I didn't see the parade but I sure's hell seen them birds," said Harvey, who had fingers or parts of fingers missing on both hands. His wild white hair stuck out in all directions. "I think them big mothers landed on the river." He licked a hand-rolled cigarette shut, striking a wooden match with his thumbnail. Verla winced, as she always did when he lit a match this way and Harvey grinned at her through the smoke. "Anybody see them land?"

"I did," Matthew said. "They were feeding down by the dam." He wished he hadn't said it, he wasn't ready to share the pelicans yet. "It's probably just a feeding stop," he added. But he knew better. Something about the decisive way they'd landed and lined up for their dinner.

"The size of those birds is something else, eh?" Wilf beamed. "I bet those things were six feet across."

"More like nine." Neil, the schoolteacher, a thin, sandy man with glasses, spoke up. "The wingspan of the white pelican is nine feet."

Wilf whistled respectfully. "Nine feet. Holy Jesus."

"And when they migrate, they navigate by the stars," Neil added.

Matthew stopped what he was doing, arrested by the picture of the big birds flying through a starry night.

The people who hadn't seen the pelicans or didn't care about them, drifted away from the table with their coffee, and chairs were scraping in the lounge, cards already slapping on the table. The tv came on, to an ad for Molson's Light. Somebody made a comment and everybody laughed.

Matthew looked at the blackboard by the kitchen door, that announced the revolving division of labour in the house. It was Matthew's and Verla's week for dishes, but Verla's name was rubbed out and Ruth's chalked in.

"I traded with Ruth. I'm going to see *The Twilight Zone*," Verla explained. "It's all cleared with Donald." Donald was the director of the house; he was seldom there after five unless there was trouble. Like last week when Harvey got drunk and fell off the third-floor fire escape, trying to sneak in. Harvey ate grass, like a dog, when he was sick, and he'd been grazing on the front lawn when Donald got there. He'd been so remorseful, Donald had given him one more chance.

"*The Twilight Zone*, eh?" Wilf said. "I hope you got somebody to hold your hand, Sunshine."

"Wouldn't you like to know?" She tweaked Wilf's beard, smiling down at him, then ran up the stairs to her room on the third floor. The sound of Verla's quick footsteps on the narrow stairs always had a strange effect on Matthew, an urge to laugh and weep at the same time. He still found it difficult to believe that this lovely child could really be an alcoholic.

Matthew scraped plates while Ruth cleared and wiped

the table. Ruby sat down with her cigarettes and note-book to plan next week's menus. The coffeemaker chugged quietly on the clean counter and the electric clock above the sink made soft little whirring sounds.

Matthew liked doing dishes. The window over the sink looked out on an apple tree that had dropped its pale blossoms on the grass — Rafe sat there now with his harmonica. With his hands immersed in hot, soapy water, he could shut out the smell of old dust in old carpets, the defeated lounge, the naked forty watt bulb in the upstairs hall. Ruth was quietly efficient, and her hair was soft and grey and didn't alarm him like Ruby's did.

Doing something like washing dishes made it easier for Matthew to talk, and he was a good listener. Ruth told him her drinking had started when her husband died, five years ago; that she wasn't going back to the little town she came from, afraid it would start all over again; that she was looking for a job. That frightened her. She had never had a job. Her two grown children didn't know what to make of any of it.

"You'll be all right," Matthew told her. "Some things just take time."

"What about you, Matthew? Do you have a family?"

"No," Matthew said. He always felt embarrassed and ashamed when someone asked him this.

He showed Ruth where things belonged, and felt sorry when he had to wring out the dishrag and hang it over the tap. Wilf would sweep and mop the floor. He wanted to ask Ruth if she'd like to go for a walk, but he didn't have the nerve.

Matthew worked as night watchman in a museum of
prairie artifacts. As he made the rounds, flashing his light
on the pampered relics, in the rooms that looked as
though the occupant had just that moment stepped out,
he walked through old rooms of his own, also kept polished and ready to occupy at a moment's notice: the wife
he had lost — he still dreamed about her sometimes —
and the home; the signpainting business he had drunk
away, the gentle, rolling countryside he'd painted so
often as background to chesty Hereford bulls, Arabian
horses, family farms; his mother, who had loved him
more than he deserved, and whose funeral he couldn't
face without a couple of stiff ones before and a hundred
more after. All gone.

And sometimes he remembered the relief of a drink
hitting his stomach, remembered only the spreading,
forgetting glow of it, and had to force himself then to
think of the hospital room. He had now gone three
months without a drink.

He always stopped at the dam on the way home from
work. There, with the waking city muted by falling
water, the morning sky flashing with gulls, and the big,
silent pelicans drifting out to feed, something eased
around Matthew's heart. As he smoked a cigarette and
drank the last of the coffee in his thermos, the doors
closed softly on those old rooms, and it was good. The
best time of the day.

He worried about the pelican that didn't seem a part
of the flock. It stayed out in the water while the others
crowded together on the small island, opening and closing their long bills to the sky now and then, for all the

world as if they were yawning. Matthew often stopped late at night on his way to work. He liked to see the island glowing whitely in the moonlight, liked knowing they were there. But even in the dark, he could often make out a single white shape apart from the rest.

August was stifling — the blistering heat pumped endlessly from some cosmic forge. The residents who slept on the steamy third floor of Hope Haven became morbid and snappish. Ruby cooked and wept and perspired. Even the narrow yard, where they gathered after supper on blankets and kitchen chairs, gave no relief till late at night, if then. As Matthew passed through the back yard on his way to work, the dim fire escape bloomed with light colored shirts and dresses, cigarettes moving like fireflies.

"Night, Matthew," they called. "Goodnight." As his tall figure passed by. "No rest for the wicked, eh, Matthew?"

Once, on his night off, he and Ruth went for a walk to the dam. When they came back, everyone but Rafe had gone out, and they sat together on the fire escape, the low, sweet notes of Rafe's harmonica drifting down from the third floor. They talked about the pelicans, the people at the house, Ruth's job hunt. They found a lot of things to laugh about. Ruth was gradually losing the sad, tired look she'd worn when she came to the house. Matthew sat a couple of steps above her, and he found it surprisingly easy to talk, his voice sounding deep and pleasant, even to himself.

"You look very nice in that shirt, Matthew." She smiled up at him. "The color suits you."

Matthew felt his face flush with pleasure. The shirt was new, and he'd hoped she would like it. He shrugged.

"Gilding the lily," he said, and they both laughed. "My mother used to say, 'Matthew isn't anything you'd want to hang on a Christmas tree, but he's a good boy'."

Ruth smiled. A sudden breeze lifted her hair, brushing it against his bare arm. It smelled like lilacs, Matthew's favorite flower.

"You are, you know. Good. A good person."

"No," said Matthew, feeling suddenly uncomfortable. And shortly after, he said he should turn in, though he lay awake for hours.

August passed. Verla decided to go back to school, and sat over books in the lounge, her brown feet bare below her faded jeans. Neil got a teaching job in a small town school and moved out. Ruth got a job in a drugstore. Ruby got around to dyeing her hair. Rafe moved a few steps closer to the others on the fire escape. A new resident — a lawyer — had a terrible seizure in the upstairs bathroom the night he moved in. Matthew saw him looking at The Last Supper, inexpertly pushed out in copper, which hung over the ugly imitation fireplace. He looked puzzled. And slowly, slowly, by an infinitesimal amount, the empty space inside Matthew got smaller.

One particularly sultry evening, Wilf and Matthew and Verla picked Ruth up from work and went for a drive. The back windows of Wilf's old car were painted over with brown paint. A relic of his drinking days, when he slept in the back seat.

"Enjoying the view back there?" Wilf laughed, as the car bounced and banged over a gravel road outside the city. Ruth sat beside Wilf, looking cool and fresh in her white uniform. Whenever they hit a hard bump, or made a left turn, Wilf's door flew open and he leaned way out to slam it shut. Ruth's hair fluttered. Dust settled in the folds of her uniform.

"Just like life, eh? This car?" Wilf shouted over his shoulder. "Ya can't look back. You gotta look ahead." He grinned at Verla in the rearview mirror. "Ain't that right, Sunshine?" The door flew open and he made a wild lunge for it. Verla was holding onto the front seat, giggling. She laughed a lot lately. "Yeah, Wilf. Whatever you say."

Ruth smiled over her shoulder at Matthew, and he realized, with a little shock of surprise, that he was having a good time. He was, in fact, having the time of his life, being shaken to pieces in Wilf's crazy old car. He even joined in when Verla started them singing.

"Feelin' good was good enough for meeeeee," Wilf sang lustily, his head thrown back, "Good enough for me an' Bobby McGee." Verla beat time on Matthew's bony knee.

When Wilf made a U turn and headed back they saw gigantic thunderclouds boiling up on the horizon. By the time they reached the city, the sky was black and the poplars along the boulevard were bent with the wind.

"Look at that sky," shouted Wilf. "Son of a gun, she's gonna pour."

"Look! Matthew, look!" Ruth pointed up over the castle-like Bessborough Hotel. The billowing slate sky was filled with soaring pelicans, their great white bodies tinged pink by the setting sun.

"Holy Jesus, look at that," Wilf said, as he swerved into a church parking lot near the Bessborough Park. As they ran across the street to the riverbank park, there was a sudden, ear-splitting crack of thunder. Verla screamed and Wilf laughed maniacally, grabbing her hand and pulling her along as the thunder rolled and rolled, like a timpani. In a grassy clearing, they stopped.

"Sweet Jumping Jesus," Wilf said softly.

Against the violent black sky, the big birds were riding the air currents. High above the glowing, golden-windowed castle, they criss-crossed in the air as if they'd rehearsed it, then half-closed their wings and dove wildly down the black sky to the rolling accompaniment of thunder. About forty feet from the ground, they pulled out of the dive and coasted back up again, their incredible white wings spread full out against the racing clouds. While the sky flashed and cracked, they rode it like a gigantic roller coaster, over and over again. Matthew looked back at the island, and saw one pelican bobbing on the green, whitecapped water.

Then, as the huge birds played their joyous game, the rain came at last, huge splats of it hitting their faces as they gazed up. Matthew felt a splash of water on his tongue, and realized that his mouth was open. As the rain came faster, Verla lifted her brown arms and twirled slowly around and around, her thin blouse soaking itself to her young breasts, as one by one the pelicans flew back downriver and made their awkward, kangaroo-hop landings on the island.

Wilf, who had actually been speechless while they watched the pelicans, now looked at Verla, beautiful in the rain, at Ruth and Matthew. His eyes were shining, and his beard streamed rivulets of rain.

"My God," he said. "I could have missed this. We all could have missed it."

And he didn't have to explain what he meant.

One morning as he came home from work, Matthew almost fell over Harvey, down on his hands and knees beside the back steps. He wasn't wearing a shirt or shoes.

"What are you doing?" asked Matthew, though he was afraid he knew. Harvey's greeenish, perspiring face peered up at him.

"Sick," mumbled Harvey.

Matthew knelt beside him, patted him awkwardly on his damp, flaccid back. He smelled sour beer and vomit.

"Why did you do it? Now they won't let you stay at the house."

"I know." Harvey sat up, wiping his mouth with some grass. "Got a smoke, Matthew?"

He lit one and put it in Harvey's mouth. Harvey dragged on it, holding it between his thumb and third finger. All the rest were missing tips, or were missing altogether.

"Aw, what the hell," he said, finally. "I got nothin' to stay sober for."

Matthew sat down, folding his long legs inside his arms. They smoked in silence, watching a sparrow stalked by a tabby cat, silent as grey mist on the grass.

"I'm sixty-two years old," Harvey said, after awhile.

"My old lady's left me. My kids don't talk to me. My drinkin' friends don't want nothin to do with me when I'm off it." He dragged on the last of the cigarette, then put it beside Matthew's foot for him to step on. He stared at some point over Matthew's shoulder. "The way I see it, there's sweet fuck-all to stay sober *for*."

Matthew couldn't think of a thing to say. They were still sitting there when Donald came to work.

Matthew helped Harvey pack, and walked him to the bus stop.

"Don't take any wooden nickels," said Harvey, as he climbed on the bus.

Matthew looked across the river one morning and saw reds and golds blooming there, noted the encroaching ochre on the green island. The flock was restless, their habits changing. They swam back and forth, no longer piling together for long periods, and they spent more time in the air, in silent, perfectly synchronized flight. Matthew worried about the one. Hoped it would have sense enough to go when the time came.

He walked with Ruth through the streets of falling leaves, began to look forward to seeing her. He worried this new thing in his life as he walked the dim corridors of the museum, flashing his light into this or that dark corner. Those other rooms, the ones he had lived in for so long, had receded slightly, as if someone had drawn a gauze curtain there. Until the night he thought of Ruth, and knew, by the sudden thrust of joy in his chest, that he loved her.

Then out they came, his Furies, from the dark corners where they had merely been biding their time. *Ugly*, they hissed in his ear. *Failure*, they whispered. *Unlovable*, they sneered. Who do you think you are, they asked, that a good woman like Ruth would be interested in you?

He sat on the running board of a Model A Ford, and pressed his hands over his ears. It wasn't safe to love. He knew that. It was dangerous, dangerous, it left you with a big hole inside. He began to shake, like a man in shock. And suddenly Matthew wanted a drink more than he had ever wanted anything in his life. When the long night was finally over, he didn't go to the dam, and he didn't go to Hope Haven.

Matthew opened his eyes to a strange room, shut them against the glaring light. Pain splintered behind his eyes, sloshed in his head when he moved. The taste of bile burned rawly from throat to stomach, and his whole body, on top of the bedspread, felt fragile as a Christmas ornament.

With a hand over his eyes, he shakily reached up and fumbled for the switch on the bedside lamp, turning it off. It was dusk. What day he didn't know. Tuesday was the last day he remembered. Where he was he didn't know, either, not even what city. He had wakened in strange cities before, and sometimes been unable to recall — ever — how he had got there.

Very carefully, he raised himself to a sitting position and lowered his feet to the floor, but the motion was too much. The room wheeled, and vomit erupted like lava just as he reached the bathroom. He heaved again and again as he cleaned up the mess. Then he realized that at some time since it all began, he had pissed his pants. On the bedspread, the large stain was still damp. Matthew sat on the floor by the bed, overcome by weakness and shame.

About two inches of whisky stood in a bottle on the table, and he shakily sipped it, gagging with the first few swallows, till the lurching things in his stomach were finally stilled. There were other, empty bottles. Carefully, then, as if he were walking on ground glass, he went to the window and looked out. The Bessborough and the river were there. There were fewer leaves — the trees across the river white and skeletal against the brown bank. He had not gone far.

Looking at the grey sky, his head pulsing with pain, he remembered something. He had wakened on the bed to the sound of geese — faint at first, like dogs barking in the distance, then closer and louder till their clangorous honking filled the night, filled the air in the room where he lay. And left him, as it receded in the distance, with the space inside larger, darker, colder than it had ever been before.

Had they gone, too? Those others? Had their beautiful black-bordered wings passed over in the night, passed powerfully, silently over the city as he lay insensible in his own piss? He must go to the river to see. He had to know, had to go to the river. He drained the bottle, felt strength and resolve flow in with the whisky.

As the cold wind hit his sweating body, he began to shake. He walked with his head down, the collar of his jacket turned up, walked with a sense of purpose, and it was still light when he arrived at the lookout.

It was empty, cold; dry leaves skittering across it. The island was deserted. Where the water spilled darkly over the dam, there was no huge, ugly bird waiting to scoop up yet another fish. Not one. He searched the grey, uncompromising sky in every direction, searched out every island. They were gone. All of them. Matthew took a deep, careful breath.

On the path to the river, sharp twigs jutted and snagged at his clothes. When he reached the place where the cement apron met the frothing water from the dam, he stopped. The river was fast and deep there. Matthew sat down to wait for dark. He remembered how he had felt before the ambulance came — the seductive sensation of peace that had stolen through him as more and more of his blood had pooled on the rooming house floor, and wondered, in an indifferent kind of way, if this would be like that.

He was wet with sweat, his jacket too light to keep out the cold, and he shook like a thin, dry pod, rattling in the wind. He smelled of urine. He wondered vaguely how many days since he had eaten, not that it mattered. He looked out at the empty island, the water, the sky. As clearly as if it had been burned into his brain, he saw the inexpressible beauty of the pelicans against the wild black sky. And he saw, as if he had been there, the silent dignity of their leaving, twenty-eight pairs of wings stroking as one through the dark, starry night.

And he thought of other things. Verla's wet brown arms as she danced in the rain, her hopeful steps on the stairs; Ruby, crying and banging pots in the big kitchen; Wilf and Rafe, and crazy, sad Harvey. Ruth. The shabby house that had, after all become a home. Staring across at the deserted brown island, Matthew waited.

Then Wilf was beside him, grabbing his arm, hanging on as if he knew he mustn't let go, even for a moment. Wilf, who must have come silently down the path and across the cement in his moccasins, though Matthew mightn't have heard him for the falling water.

"Hey, Matthew, hey man. I don't believe it! Holy shit, am I glad to see you!" His little eyes gleaming in the dusk. "We've been down here a hundred times, looking for you." He was holding on with both hands, pulling at Matthew, pulling him painfully to his feet, Matthew allowing it, too weak to get away, even from little Wilf.

Wilf pushed Matthew ahead of him, toward the path.

"God, I really don't believe this. We thought you were in the river. Goddam it, why'd you hafta do that? What happened you had to go get drunk? Eh?"

Wilf pushed faster as the words came faster. Matthew stumbled. "Sorry." Helping him up. Pushing him on.

"You're crazy, you know, I got a good notion to kick your skinny ass into the middle of next week." Pushing with his hand on the small of Matthew's back. "And you don't smell like Chanel Number Five, either. Is that what you want?"

"It's been godawful around the house . . . Ruby bawling her head off and cooking worse shit than ever . . . Ruth looking for you everywhere, and shut up in her room the resta the time." Somewhere, under the sickness that threatened to collapse him right there on the path, Matthew registered that. "Verla, too. Missed an exam out lookin' for you."

167

"And you were just going to jump in the river, weren't you? Well, if you ever take another drink you won't hafta jump because I'll fucking well throw you in . . . You hear?" Matthew heard, but it took everything he had to just keep putting one foot ahead of the other on the steep slope.

Wilf stopped to sneeze, and Matthew stood swaying like a tree.

"Five days of chasing around to bars and freezing my ass off down here. I've got a cold and it's your fault." And so on it went, all the way up the path.

They were waiting by Wilf's old car, Ruth's white uniform the first thing Matthew saw when he came over the rise. The joy in her face. Verla's smile. "Everybody in the car!" Wilf shouted like a general. And they got in the back seat as Wilf got Matthew into the front, running around and leaping into the driver's seat as if Matthew might escape before he got there. Matthew hadn't the strength to turn the handle.

Wilf turned and grinned at the others. "Well, here he is. Here's Matthew." He smacked the steering wheel and yelled, "*Son of a bitch, we found him!*"

Matthew's head splintered. Over his shoulder, Verla's smile lit up the back of the car.

"Thank God," said Ruth, in her quiet voice.

For a moment, there was silence. Then Verla reached for him, hugging his ugly, whiskery face to her smooth cheek, and he felt her tears, wet on his face. "Oh, Matthew. We were so scared."

"Scared shitless," Wilf agreed, his grin threatening to split his face. "Have you had enough?" he asked,

giving Matthew's shoulder a shake. Matthew thought
he would pass out. Then Wilf scooted across the seat
and put his arms around Matthew, too.

"I've never been in so fucking many bars in my whole
fucking life," he said, starting to laugh. "Isn't that
right?" he asked them, and they all laughed, agreeing
with him. "Every grungy bar in town," said Verla, and
they laughed some more. Ruth reaching for him, too.
All of them touching, holding him in an awkward tangle.
He was chilled through and they contained his shaking
with their bodies, paid no attention to his silence.

Suddenly from deep inside Matthew, from the empty
place where he had lived for so long, the sobs erupted,
tearing at his throat with their violence, jolting his thin
body over and over. No one said "don't", they just let
him. And held him, and warmed him, and breathed on
him.

"Oh, God," he said, finally, his voice sounding
hoarse, unused. "Oh, God."

And he opened his arms and let them in.

9001971

Simmie, Lois
Pictures

Wapiti

JUL   1993